CW00801734

The Triangle

Ed Adams

a firstelement production

Ed Adams

First published in Great Britain in 2009 by bubbleandsqueek
Published in Great Britain in 2020 by first element
Directed by the six twenty

Copyright © 2009 rashbre
Copyright © 2020 Ed Adams

10 9 8 7 6 5 4 3

All rights reserved.
No part of this publication may be reproduced, stored in a retrieval
system, or transmitted, in any form or by any means, without the
prior permission in writing of the publisher, nor be otherwise
circulated in any form or binding or cover other than that in which it is
published and without a similar condition including this condition
being imposed on the subsequent purchaser.

Every effort has been made to acknowledge the appropriate
copyright holders. The publisher regrets any oversight and will be
pleased to rectify any omission in future editions.

Similarities with real people or events is unintended and
coincidental.

A CIP catalogue record for this book is available from the British
Library.

ISBN : 978-1-9163383-2-6

Ebook ISBN : 978-1-9163383-3-3

Printed and bound in Great Britain by
Ingram Spark

Ed Adams
an imprint of first element
rashbre@mac.com

PART ONE

Don't let it get to you

A wise person should have money in their head,
but not in their heart. –
Jonathan Swift

Ed Adams

Art for art's sake?

The white cube's sterile tranquillity gave no clue of the impending violence. Lucien took the programme for this Sloane Square gallery to orient himself. The white rooms serially displayed cutting edge art. Very different from the place he'd visited the last time he'd received private tickets. That had been a rather grim gallery the size and appearance of a newsagent's, somewhere out west — Graffiti art, decomposing artefacts on the floor and rats running free as part of the installation.

Not this time. It was clean pictures on clean walls in a gallery which Lucien had pretty much to himself. He looked towards the white space between the hanging pictures.

Pristine.

Then he noticed it from the corner of his eye. A fragile red line was arcing across the wall. A second line appeared as he looked at it. Then he felt it. The knife had done serious damage.

Then he felt nothing.

Outside, November graphite skies, gentle rain. A quiet,

smartly dressed woman slowly left the gallery, flicked her umbrella up and walked across to a modern metallic BMW. The driver clicked the locks, she climbed into the back seat, and the vehicle slipped into the heavy traffic.

Hours later, across town, Jake Lambers was walking to the pub. He'd had a tough day. The boss had torn him off a strip about the expenses from his recent trip to Liverpool. He'd been trying to get "an exclusive" with a singer who was supposed to be "seeing" a footballer. It would have made an excellent insider piece, but the trip was doomed because he'd received incorrect information. Instead, he'd made the best of a lousy job in a lively city with a great nightlife. The expenses had only just arrived and, upon reflection, seemed excessive, mainly because there was no story. So now he was going to meet Bigsy and Clare to drown his sorrows.

The pub in Westminster was buzzing. There were no tables and pretty much a mob standing by the bar. It was early evening, and the local offices had tipped out into the neighbourhood, and the inevitable 'one before the train' ritual was in full flood.

"Jake, Jake – here!" called Bigsy – whose real name was Dave but had adopted Bigsy on account of his size and didn't mind this affectionate but somewhat politically incorrect nickname.

Bigsy had commandeered a prime corner spot at the bar and standing with him was Clare. They were well into their second drinks of the early evening. Bigsy had spotted Jake the moment he'd entered the bar in customary journalist semi-smart clothing, dark jacket and an open-necked white shirt.

"Can dress it up or dress it down", Jake had once explained. Bigsy was pleased to see Jake; he, Clare and Jake were the nuclei of a gang of friends who often met and attended many social functions together.

"Let's go to the Crown," said Bigsy, "this place is heaving!" As he spoke, Jake's phone rang – he knew it rang because it vibrated – you couldn't hear the phone above the pub noise.

"Just a minute," called Jake as he reversed out of the side door of the pub, back onto the busy street near Westminster tube. Only then did he notice the number – Mark, one of his other drinking buddies.

"Jake, it's Mark. Have you heard already? We've just been called about Lucien. He's been killed, at an art gallery."

Heavy traffic was passing, mainly a stream of buses and taxis. Jake couldn't take in this conversation. Was he hearing it badly because of the traffic or was it a wind up?

"Mark – are you pissed? This doesn't make sense!"

Mark repeated what he had said previously. To Jake, it felt like one of those occasions where he'd had to sober up suddenly when something big was about to go down after chucking-out time, except this time he wasn't drunk.

Jake started to take in that what he was hearing was true. Lucien had been murdered. Lucien, who he'd been with a few days previously. Jake watched as Clare backed out of the pub, pushing the door slowly with her hip, whilst still holding a glass of something. She caught Jake's eye and waited a few steps away from him.

"Jake – what is it? You look in shock!" she said in a teasing voice wagging a finger of her spare hand towards him because he'd only just arrived and then left them for his cell-phone. Jake noticed her expression change as she became aware that Jake was looking unusually grave.

Jake continued the conversation with Mark for a few moments longer and could see Clare listening and piecing together the fragments she could hear of the conversation. As he hung up, he looked towards Clare to begin to tell her.

"I think I heard most of it," she started to say. Jake knew Clare was smart and that she would very likely have figured out what had happened even from only hearing part of one side of the conversation.

"I'll get Bigsy," she continued, "you can tell us both together." Clare strode back into the pub and a few moments later the three of them were standing together on the pavement as Jake relayed the news from Mark about Lucien's murder. Jake said he'd agreed to go to visit Mark to get further information.

"Let's go," said Bigsy.

By this time, at the gallery, a full crime scene had been established. The detective in charge, Detective Inspector Trueman, had walked into what he knew was a professional hit. This crime scene wasn't casual violence; it was a clinically executed assassination. There was no weapon to see, but the precision of the knife was medical. To his surprise, Trueman had found himself thinking that the red arcs across the wall almost looked like part of the art exhibition.

Radios crackled, police forensics operated, cameras whined (they used to click, he thought, but now they've gone digital you hear the flash recharging more than the whirring sounds from the old motor drives). There was blue and white police tape — a lot of it. The white cube now looked messy, distorted and unclean.

"What is the story?" asked Trueman of the medical examiner checking the sprawled body.

"Quick version", replied the medic, "This was professional; fast, but with a lot of deliberate blood spill. Someone wanted this to get someone else very annoyed. I can tell you the usual things about the height and weight of assassin – probably a woman, by the way, but this looks like something from martial arts."

Trueman's assistant was Sergeant Andy Green. They had worked together for around three years and knew how each other operated. Trueman gestured to Green, "And what do we know about the victim?"

Green began to search the body, "er...Recent suit from Marks and Spencer; M&S tie too; this could all be a matching set." From one bloodied pocket he pulled out a driving license. "Lucien Deschamps - lives in Hampstead," he read from the card. "Normal bank cards, nothing special. There's an oyster card in here too, so he's probably a regular commuter. Seems to work in a corporate travel group according to this business card. Quite honestly, there's nothing out of the ordinary."

The processing continued, and Trueman called his station.

"We're coming in", he said, "We need to get some sense around this situation. A lot of people know about this already, what with this being a Press day at the gallery. It is impossible to stop the general news getting out, but I want us to keep anything else we find under wraps for a few more hours. If this is a serious crime, we need to decide how we want to release any findings."

Trueman looked across to Green and gestured with his eyes, "let's go", he called, and Green nodded back in agreement. Green was a modern law enforcer, DNA, CCTV, profiling, all part of the contemporary way. Trueman was more traditional, though respectful of modern techniques; he'd been through the various modernisation courses along the way but still had a strong belief in basic policing methods. They made a good team, because they complemented one another in the way they thought about cases.

By the time they reached the nearby Chelsea police station, Trueman had already called to obtain a search of police files for anything on Deschamps as well as basic enquiries with his employer and some general bank statements and phone bills. Nothing showed circumstances out of the ordinary. There didn't appear to be anything special about the victim.

"So, was the assassin clever at covering tracks?" queried Green, "or did the professional get the wrong person?" he suggested.

"I think we can rule out random violence," responded Trueman, "This was done by a cold-blooded professional killer, almost certainly a hit for someone."

"Maybe there was someone else in the gallery who was the real target? Or perhaps it is linked with the exhibition or owners?" ventured Green.

Trueman knew these were a long shots or mere guesses because most times a professional hitman would stake a victim for some time before making their move unless this was a request for sudden and violent action by someone, as yet, unknown. Trueman's time in the force meant he had come across some strange and twisted behaviours and much violence, but this one was giving him a powerful sensation which almost felt like personal danger.

Trueman and Green had looked through the records for who had appeared for this private viewing. The irony was that it was not even the main private viewing. The day was to get the artwork arranged and to invite the press to preview before the main event started. It meant there was hardly anyone at the gallery. Attendees were spinning through fast for impressions to write in their chosen media. The exhibiting artist was tucked away in a suite at the Dorchester like a film star handling successive repetitive interviews.

The razzmatazz of the exhibition was planned to start on Wednesday, some two days after the bloody incident.

Except now there had been a block put on the start by the police. A gallery filled with blue and white tape, police officers and the aftermath of serious crime didn't make for a good show unless it was some sort of warped installation piece.

Walking through walls

Late afternoon near Deauville, Northern France and a little Cessna plane landed smoothly. It taxied towards an edge of the small but rather exclusive airport. A dark Mercedes saloon waited while a woman climbed out of the flight. The driver shook hands with the woman who got into the back of the car which edged quietly away. The pilot busied himself with plane checking procedures in the closing light of a surprisingly pleasant November evening.

A little later, the same car pulled up at a distinguished hotel, which looked like a Norman manor. The passenger left the vehicle and, carrying no luggage, walked directly to the elevators and towards a room in the hotel.

In London, Jake, Bigsy and Clare had grabbed a cab to Mark's. Of them all, Mark was probably the staunchest friend of Lucien, and they had known one another for many years. Jake, Bigsy and Clare decided it was respectful to let Jake relay the news in more detail to Mark, alone. Bigsy knew a nearby pub, so he and Clare left Jake at Mark's door and walked the few yards to the pub.

Bigsy quickly scoped the room and selected a corner table. He and Clare made to claim it by depositing coats and then Bigsy approached the bar to order the drinks. Clare sat waiting, noting a strong slightly sweet-smelling aroma from the immediate surroundings. Bigsy returned, and they looked at one another.

"I know," said Clare, "I think its jasmine." They looked around, and then Clare pointed to a small white box at the same height as the music speakers. "There it is," she pointed.

"How American", said Bigsy "We can't go to a bar now without having perfume squirted at us; now if it was chips and whisky..." Bigsy trailed off. They sat in silence for a few seconds, except for the noise of Bigsy opening some 'flamed steak' potato crisps and spreading the opened packet on the dark oak table between them.

"...That news about Lucien was terrible," Bigsy eventually continued. Bigsy and Clare's eyes locked in agreement. They both had similar views about Lucien.

Bigsy tested the way he could say it, "He was a nice enough guy, but, er, quite quiet. I always found him pretty intense, and this could make him hard work for a whole evening".

Clare nodded agreement. "I think he was a little bit afraid of me or something. Not just shy. He didn't seem to find it very easy to talk to me and always looked as if he was getting ready to make apologies to move on."

They both knew that Lucien usually looked a little reserved and formal in his choice of clothes and general style. He always wore a suit to work, and when they'd been out with him, it had usually been with him along as an accessory to an event selected by Jake or Mark. Lucien had nearly always come along alone and often still in his' work clothes'.

Bigsy and Clare thought of Lucien mainly as Jake's friend. In the chain of social friendships, Lucien knew Mark well. Jake also knew Mark well, and Lucien would sometimes show up at Jake's social occasions. They'd all been for drinks together occasionally although Jake, Clare and Bigsy had regarded

Lucien as something of an outsider at social events. Lucien was pleasant but didn't enter the spirit of their 'in-jokes' nor take the lead in the conversation. Lucien did seem to have done well for himself, living in Hampstead, which pretty much guaranteed him a smart address, but in reality, he was in a house converted from a larger house into a number of expensively priced little boxes.

Bigsy continued, "I can't really see why anyone would do that to Lucien. He's got to be a victim of some kind of accident or mistake. Lucien's not exactly a risk taker."

Clare nodded. "Yes, Lucien's highlights seemed to involve stories about things that happened on his bus ride to work."

Both Bigsy and Clare thought Lucien completely under exploited where he lived, both in terms of the immediate environment and also the lack of use he made of his easy access to all of central London.

If he'd been alive, Clare and Bigsy would have privately labelled Lucien a loser, but because he was a friend of Jake and he was now dead, they owed the loyalty of support to Jake.

"So, will we stick around here tonight?" asked Bigsy, "or head back North" – It was only to Finsbury Park in North London, but they were near to Gloucester Road, on the edges of fashionable Kensington in west London at the moment. Clare shrugged her answer, "Whatever – I think we're all going to be calling in sick tomorrow at this rate."

Clare's job was expendable. She'd been seeing a different friend of Jake's for a long time, got to know a lot of Jake's crowd and then when she'd had a major break up had decided to stay around Jake, who always seemed to have good things happening. She was between men right now and hung out with Bigsy (purely platonic) and Jake (why spoil a good thing?).

Clare's real interest was to get into TV or radio, and the other jobs she had were really time markers until she could crack the media formula. She was quite a good actress and had been in some lesser roles in stage productions and her other day work was really what she considered to be "between roles", but one up from bar-work or waitressing. Clare was also very interested in 'backstage' roles and production and in her heart she knew she'd probably wind up there rather than on stage or in front of the cameras, but that would still do nicely.

Jake's crowd had been a real find because Jake worked for a magazine and seemed to interview all kinds of interesting people, admittedly usually C-list types, but C-list with access, nonetheless. This gave her more of the ever-essential 'contacts' as she sought ways to further herself in 'show-biz'.

Clare's original slightly mercenary interest in Jake's friends had flipped into a true friendship with the group when she'd broken up with her last boyfriend. When she first lived in London, she'd been in a nasty flat around Elephant and Castle. Then she'd moved in with Steve until he drove her nuts and then she didn't have anywhere to stay. Using the Evening Standard to find a new flat was ridiculous; they walked off the page as fast as they were advertised. Word of mouth was the only answer.

Jake and his friends had rallied round, found her a temporary room in Bigsy's place (which he shared with two other fellas) and then moved her into a new nearby flat that a friend was leaving somewhat better than the place she'd left in the Elephant and Castle. They'd bailed her out on rent for a couple of weeks and then she'd got the new job – which paid well but was mind-numbingly boring creating photographic images for corporate leaflets. The joke was that the fees she could charge for taking a photograph, tweaking the colours and then merging it into a document with some text was obscene and Clare thought this was a quick way to pay off some debts and get solvent again.

Bigsy's job was semi-manual. He repaired company computer networks as a 'geek in a van' – except he used his cherished, though slightly scruffy, Rover car. Mainly he was a freelance addition to various large companies who needed something repaired at a diverse location. Half the time this meant driving somewhere, pulling the plug out of the back, counting to ten, plugging it back in and everything worked. Sometimes it was more complicated and Bigsy really did know how computers worked, so he could fix most things. Tomorrow, if he didn't go to his client in 'out west' in Andover, he might just have to phone them and tell them the unplugging trick, although once he'd done that, his supply of repeat business may tail off from that particular organization.

Jake was the common link that had introduced Bigsy, Lucien, Clare and Mark. Jake was a pretty well-established journalist and had his own by-line in the monthly magazine that was his main source of income. In addition, he did freelance work for other publications and this veered from the Guardian through to the advertising flyers handed out free on the Heathrow Express.

Jake had been writing in newspapers and magazines pretty much since school. He'd edited a school broadsheet, then at University ran a music magazine (which also let him get into many gigs without paying) and then after a rather odd dalliance with a fishing magazine, he'd moved into more cutting edge urban style magazines, which was where he worked now.

'Street' was the current magazine. Strong readership, internet profile, good advertising and viewed as a foreteller of the next big thing. That's how the graffiti artist show with the rats had first appeared, after Jake saw the early signs of the admittedly classy graffiti around the streets of east London. Bizarrely, Lucien had accompanied Jake to the show a few weeks earlier and appeared very interested, which is the reason Jake passed the free tickets from the private viewing to Lucien a week or so ago.

There was a buzzing sound from the table in the pub. Both Bigsy and Clare looked down to where their drinks were stood. It was Bigsy's phone that was buzzing and ever so slightly moving across the table. Grim faced, Bigsy lifted it to his ear.

"Come over," said the voice, "Mark's given me the low-down – I think there may be more to this than it seems. Let's leave for tonight but I think I may need some help tomorrow." Bigsy nodded to Clare. She already knew they'd all be spending time on this tomorrow.

"Okay," replied Bigsy, downing the remains of his beer and delicately picking up the last two crisps, "but let's go back to my place so that we are all ready for an early start tomorrow."

At the same moment, in Deauville, France, the well-dressed woman slid her key into the electronic lock of her hotel room. She walked in, closed the door quietly and flicked the deadlock. She crossed the room past the bed and stood near to the balcony, which looked out to the sea.

Near to the side of the bed, there was another door, the type that is used to make two adjacent rooms in a hotel link together. She twisted the door lock and opened her door, revealing another door belonging to the adjoining room. She pushed on the second door, which opened immediately. She softly closed both doors, locking the one for the new room she had entered.

Inside the room she looked towards the bed and then picked up the nearest pillow. She felt inside it and retrieved a large envelope. Without further examination, in one movement she stepped towards the door of the new room, quietly opened it and after checking both ways, made her way back into the hotel corridor. If she was stopped, she could say that she had been asked to carry the unopened envelope by someone else.

A few minutes later she stepped into an Italian registered Alfa Romeo. She flicked on the headlights, briefly revved the engine and then pulled out of the hotel and headed for the Autoroute.

The Interview

A noisy kitchen scene, Capital Radio burbling, coffee machine fizzing and an occasional bang from some bacon fried on too high heat. Bigsy, with a cooking spatula in one hand, was already on the telephone. "Thanks, mate- I owe you for this one".

Bigsy had been on the phone to James, a friend and fellow computer geek who had a well-paid job in a city Bank. Bigsy had just persuaded James to take a day off from work and to make the journey to Andover to look at whatever it was that was broken.

James would need to say he was from Bigsy's outfit and was more than happy to help Bigsy. A month earlier, Bigsy had helped James out on a personal matter that called for a man with some bulk, following a problem with a motor car purchase by James. That very vehicle could now be used by James to help dig Bigsy out of an inconvenient appointment.

The previous night, when they had returned to Bigsy's, Jake had relayed the story of Lucien to Bigsy and Clare over a couple of bottles of wine. Bigsy and Clare had decided to help out in what seemed to be a scary and somewhat complicated situation. Jake and Clare had both decided it was easiest to simply stay at Bigsy's overnight, especially after two bottles of red wine, on top of the earlier evening's consumption.

The hissing and popping sound from the bacon and scrambled eggs reminded Bigsy of the breakfast, which he was assembling in the kitchen. "If we're going to be wandering around all day, we'll need something inside us," he mused to no-one in particular.

Clare had scrunched her hair and was still wearing the same clothes, which she somehow had made look different for what was a continuation of the previous day.

Bigsy, by comparison, appeared to be demonstrating the art of deterioration, with new grease spatters from the cooking on what was once a white tee-shirt emblazoned with "iBurn" and a picture of a smoking computer.

"Let's get Jake; we need to get started," he commented to Clare.

"Jake!" he shouted, "C'mon! It's going to be a busy one". He flipped the first portion of the intriguing-looking breakfast into a plate and handed it to Clare.

Clare slightly wrinkled her nose but remembered from her previous stint staying at Bigsy's that whatever it looked like, it usually tasted pretty good.

Jake's story from last night set anticipation with both Clare and Bigsy. Clare always thought Lucien had lived on a different planet from Jake and the rest of Jake's clan, but at a time like this would hold these thoughts private. The part Jake told them the previous evening meant they would expect today to be pretty eventful.

The door clicked open, and Jake walked into the kitchen. Wet hair from a shower, a new, oversized tee-shirt emblazoned with 'Siouxsie' from Bigsy's wardrobe and dark rings under his eyes which indicated he'd not slept much.

"Sorry about the shirt - but it will look great under your jacket," said Bigsy, "Here's some Maison Bigsy breakfast, now let's go over your story again!"

Jake scraped a wooden chair and sat, beginning to explain the last few days and the part that Lucien had inadvertently played.

He began, "I was supposed to report on the art show for the magazine but passed them to Lucien when we were out at the Builder's Arms a few days ago. Lucien had been to that graffiti show with me and seemed to enjoy it, so I thought this could be a 'win-win'."

Jake took a piece of the bacon from his plate by two fingers and placed it between a slice of unbuttered bread. Then he flipped the lid on some brown sauce and dribbled a small amount over the improvised sandwich.

"I figured that if Lucien could get me a catalogue and maybe describe a few of the things he spotted in the visit over a quick beer, then I could write the review 'blind'. That way I could scoot over to the Dorchester, get ten minutes with the artist and 'bing'!"

Bigsy was eyeing the remnants of Jake's plate after the sandwich-making operation. Ever so delicately, he slid the plate to one side, as if clearing it away.

"I don't think I'd told anyone else about what I'd done," continued Jake, "It was supposed to give Lucien a preview of the show and me a chance to get the story without quite as much running around."

"So whatever happened to Lucien could have been aimed at you?" questioned Clare. Jake had hinted at this last night, but Clare had been slow to accept this somewhat paranoid theory. It all seemed too implausible, except that Lucien was dead, but that also seemed unbelievable.

"Nice egg, is it?" questioned Jake to Bigsy, who was just finishing the remnants of Jake's plate.

"Mmm", said Bigsy, "...But I thought with murders and mysteries there was supposed to be a motive? You are not exactly Mr Big League gangster!" he smiled towards Jake.

Jake had stayed awake pretty much all of the previous night. He'd been a journalist long enough to know that a good article needed an angle, a motivation. When he interviewed someone, and it didn't stack up, he had acquired a good sense that something was missing. He called it 'evidence' which was not supposed to sound like a criminal investigation but had some of the same techniques.

Jake continued "I've been thinking about Lucien and the killing a lot. I really do think it must be something to do with me. I promise you both that I'm not involved with anything truly dodgy and I'd tell you both if there was something bad that I'd done, especially when it's something like this."

Bigsy and Clare both nodded. They knew Jake well and could read him if he lied, like the time he'd borrowed Clare's leather jacket and then somehow lost it in a club. Jake was professional for his work but transparent to both Bigsy and Clare.

"So here's my partial theory", said Jake as he sipped the freshly brewed coffee. "I've been working on a lifestyle piece called 'fast boys' about twenty-somethings who drove exotic fast supercars. The interviewees were mainly pop stars, footballers and the occasional mobile phone salesman with his own business. I had interviewed several Ferrari and Lamborghini owners and then gone to see a guy named Darren Collins, who owned a particularly expensive McLaren supercar which was apparently one of only several in the world. It's amazing how many of these guys there are in central London alone. See how some of the underground car parks are crammed full of Porsche, Astons these supercars."

"I had to go to an office in South London, just over Tower

Bridge. You know the area before you get to Southwark and Borough Market. It's all recently renovated area with old warehouses made good. Bermondsey, I guess you'd call it."

Bigsy and Clare nodded. They'd both been to parties in the area.

"The neighbourhood was well-heeled and had fashion house headquarters in the nearby streets. Typical 'American film about London Town territory' but still only a few streets away from the rough scenes in 'Lock, Stock and Two Smoking Barrels'."

"Sounds like a walk-fast area", interrupted Bigsy.

"More or less", continued Jake, "At least a 'be careful at night' zone. Anyway, I'd been waiting in the office for Darren, who was late for our meeting. I was sitting in a ground floor meeting room with a glass wall and slatted blinds. They had good coffee, and I'd already finished the first cup while waiting for Darren. I was about to grab another cup when there was a noise outside the room, several people, softly spoken English but with a foreign accent."

"The accents sounded middle eastern. I wasn't paying a lot of attention to begin with, just waiting for a chance to refill my coffee without disturbing anyone. But then, call it my journalistic instincts rather than nosey parker; I decided to see what was happening just in case it would add some depth to the interview."

Jake explained he had left the door of the meeting room open so that he could get a warning of Darren Collin's approach, and this had helped him hear what was happening.

"The conversation was something to do with international trade and payments. I switched on my little old-school Olympus recorder when I started to pay attention to the conversation. The talking actually went on for quite a long time, maybe fifteen minutes. It had started softly but got

25

louder and louder and then suddenly stopped. I decided to grab another coffee to give me a glimpse of what was happening."

Jake looked at Clare and Bigsy who were taking in the whole of his story.

"As I walked from the meeting room, I startled the people who had been talking and were now getting ready to leave. To be honest, they startled me, too, because I thought they were sitting in an adjacent room. There were five men in total. Three Arabic looking people in dark suits, a very tall guy with cropped hair, dark tan and what seemed to be a dark green suit and a fifth person who turned out to be Darren Collins."

"We were together in the entrance area to the office suite. Their group carried on making its way towards the door and I made a beeline for the coffee. Out of the corner of my eye, I saw the tall person with the unusual suit peel off from the group and come towards me."

"Mr Collins will be with you in a few minutes", the green suit said with a strong southern American accent. "We have just finished – Do you mind if I have one of your business cards", he asked, "I know that Mr Collins would want to recommend you to my colleagues", he continued.

Jake had been surprised by this, he'd never met this group before, had no idea why Darren Collins would have recommended him to anyone, but hey, maybe there was some freelance business available. He'd swapped cards with the American.

Jake continued the story to Clare and Bigsy, "A few moments later, Darren returned, and we returned to the meeting room where I'd been sitting to start the lifestyle interview. Darren appeared smartly dressed; suit, no tie, crisp white shirt. Sort of expensive city trader look with some discreet bling, if you know what I mean. I'd normally have a picture, but no photographer for this trip because as the article was about the fast car, the photoshoot was handled separately."

Jake looked briefly at Clare and Bigsy. Clare had finished the breakfast provided by Bigsy and was now scribbling a few notes based upon what Jake was saying. It appeared to be on the inside of a cereal packet.

Jake continued, "Collins seemed preoccupied during the interview, which was also quite obvious. He didn't seem to be very interested in talking about the car, which is unusual; normally, someone with a super special car wants to flaunt it to show how great they think they are. Although Collins didn't seem to care about most of the interview, there was just one area where he emphasized what he was saying."

Jake explained that he thought maybe Darren Collins was trying to project a version of 'cool', but it seemed the previous meeting rattled him.

"I'll come back to the moment in the interview, but the next part is why I think everything may be linked. A week or so after the interview, well before the story was due, my editor called me. He told me that Darren Collins had been killed in a road accident. The section of the story covering Darren Collins was being replaced with a twenty-something golfer with a Dodge Viper. 'Street' wouldn't still write about 'fast boys' if one of them had just died. There wasn't going to be an alternative story about Collins, so in 'Street' terms, the interview was no longer relevant."

Clare commented, "This does all seem to link together with what's happened to Lucien. How come you didn't think of this earlier?"

Jake replied, "There's always something happening when involved in this type of journalism. The nature of celebrity and wannabe means people are getting arrested for airline tantrums, too much booze and pills and the occasional car crash or similar.

"It's like the wallpaper of the B-listers. So Collins' tragic accident was more of an inconvenience in the newsgathering world. It affected my quota more than anything else. I'll admit it knocked me back when I first heard, but I hardly warmed to the guy, and he seemed to be off in his own world anyway."

Clare and Bigsy nodded as Jake continued, "I suppose if I'd paid more attention, then I might have connected the dots.

"I sort of regarded this as a dead story, and to be honest, I was also in some trouble from that trip I made to Liverpool."

Bigsy laughed, "...that trip. I'm not surprised- I think we all thought you'd get the boot after that example of expense account creativity!"

Jake had found several clubs and expensive hotels on his otherwise wasted visit. He'd decided to take 'wasted' in an altogether different direction.

"So when I got back to London, I was told by the office that someone had made several calls to the main switchboard and visited a couple of times looking for me. The description was of a tall American, short hair and suntan, looked vaguely military. It could only be the guy I'd met at Darren Collins' office, although the business card left with the office was for a different company. Eventually, I checked the names, and in both cases, it was Chuck Manners."

Clare stifled a laugh. "No, that's not a real name. It can't be. Chuck Manners."

"He looked as if he could 'chuck' me across a room," responded Jake.

Bigsy was fussing around with the remaining bacon, which had somehow congealed in the frying pan. He looked over and said,

"So if we add it all together, there is a story. The meeting with

Darren Collins, the overheard conversation. The strange behaviour of Chuck the green-suited American. The death of Collins and the visits of the American to your office.

"Plus the different business cards and now the murder of Lucien, who was standing in for you at the art show. These things can't all be a coincidence!"

"I agree," said Clare,

"I was also thinking about this last night. To begin with I just thought you were in shock about Lucien and some of your journalistic imagination was coming through in the way you looked at the situation.

"But now I've had a chance to take it in, and I think you may have a point."

Clare scraped the kitchen chair across the floor and sat closer to Jake. "Look, I've listed some of the points". She scanned the list she'd made on the cereal box. The list comprised:

Visit Collins
Overhear Arabs
Get American business card
Meet Collins
Collins dies in a car crash
American shows up at Jake's office
Lucien takes your tickets to the art show
Lucien murdered

Clare had now retrieved some paper from a drawer in Bigsy's kitchen. She knew her way around the flat from the time she'd spent crashed there when Jake and Bigsy had helped her out earlier in the year.

"Okay, Jake, you'll need to take this to the police, but you still haven't told us about the thing that Collins emphasized during the interview. What can you remember?"

Jake went on to explain. "When I went to interview Collins, I'd also noticed the general look of the office. It was modern, clean-lined, stylish and minimalist. A designer had created it with taste, and budget limits didn't seem to have been any concern. Trust me, I know cutting edge cool, and Darren's office was a pretty good approximation.

"But the other thing that struck me was the complete lack of industriousness in what seemed to be a high-worth empire. For Darren to be turning the kind of money he appeared to be, there had to be some kind of activity to support it. I visit plenty of offices for interviews and client shoots and this was by far the most impressive looking, but the least busy. Something looked wrong, and the phrase 'shell company' was flickering through my mind while I sipped the coffee."

"Also, as the conversation with the middle eastern gentlemen became noisier I'd heard them talk about some kind of problem with the way Collins had been operating 'the clearances'. The quietly spoken Arab gentleman was politely advising him that the contract would close if he was unable to regain sufficient control. The American had emphasized this point as the group were about to break up. That was about the time when I pretended to wander out to get the coffee refill."

At the time Jake had just regarded this argument as the hustle-bustle of busy commerce. Still, he also thought (maybe politically incorrectly) that there may be some carpet bazaar bargaining going on as well.

"...and guys," continued Jake, "...there is another reason I think this may be more complicated, and that I may be in some danger."

Nothing leads South

At the Chelsea Police station, Trueman had been going through standard police procedures for this case. A cold-blooded killing, more like an execution than any random violence. No sign of theft and no real crime scene evidence leading towards the killer.

They had started using routine procedures to look at records for any similar crimes seeking advice from police army forensics about the style and precision of the wound that had been the inflicted.

There was nothing obvious, except the view that this was a professional hit.

Furthermore, there was no discernible motive and no witnesses. There was camera footage from the gallery, but the room where the crime took place had suffered a defective camera for the last day. The gallery owner had said they'd never had any trouble previously at the gallery and the cameras in the entrance were the most useful for general surveillance. There was a call out to get the broken camera fixed, but the outfit repairing it had said it would be better to replace the unit, which appeared to have shattered inside. The repair was scheduled in time for the public opening, but not for the press preview. As a result, there was nothing captured of the crime although they did have clear footage of everyone visiting the gallery on the day of the incident.

They'd already combed the video for the entire day as well as the nearby street surveillance from a bus lane, a jeweller's and a couple of fashion stores. Many of the people entering and leaving the gallery were recognized, were employees or members of the trade press. After Lucien's entry, there had been a couple of further visitors, and shortly after the incident a couple of people managed to leave before the arrival of police, ambulance and others associated by the crime investigators.

Everyone leaving tallied except for one man picked up on the bus lane camera getting into a BMW. They had a number plate for the car, but it was a fake, cloned from a Vauxhall Astra still on a dealer forecourt in South London.

They were trying to trace the car's route, picking it up on other cameras, but even with Congestion Charge and traffic management cameras, it was long, laborious and painstaking work. Coupled with the other aspects of the killer's professionalism, they expected the car would have disappeared somewhere not far from the original scene.

The passenger of that BMW was by now a long way from London. Driving from Deauville to the Cote d'Azur was a long journey, across the whole landmass of France. The driver followed her sat-nav but had pre-planned to use Autoroutes for almost the entire journey, taking a reasonably direct autoroute bypassing Paris, Lyon, Valance and Aix which was many hundreds of kilometres of driving.

She briefly looked down at her Irish passport, which she would be using for this journey. Brophy. Amelia Brophy.

After Paris, the road had cleared, and she was making good time, staying within the speed limits to avoid being timed by police on long section between the tolls.

Sometimes a route on normal roads ran parallel to the Autoroutes. Still, she maintained her speed and focus on the journey, eventually pulling off at services ostensibly to refuel, but first parking in a row of mixed registration cars from Great Britain, France, Germany and Holland. She was looking for a blue Peugeot saloon and parked a couple of rows from it but with a direct view to it. She blipped another key on her keyring, seeing the locks in the Peugeot's car door rise and then fall again as she re-locked the car.

The next services, with its adjacent hotel, would be fine for the overnight stop, except she'd be in the blue car instead of the red one.

Picking up just the hotel envelope from the car, she walked across to the services shop, bought an apple and some bottled water and after a few minutes pause made her way back to the parking lot and into the Peugeot. It was a diesel and had enough range to get the rest of the way to Cannes, without stopping.

She sat in the car and looked at the envelope she'd picked up back in Deauville. Now she was far enough away to open it. To her surprise, there were two items inside instead of the one she had expected. The first a photocopy of a banker's draft in Swiss francs for a considerable sum of money, made out to her, with her real name. The second was a photocopied sheet of A4, with a selection of photographs of Jake, a series of addresses and phone numbers.

She realized the message she was seeing. She was not getting paid. Her target was still active, and the person she had killed in the gallery must have been someone else. This situation was extremely irregular and increased her risks considerably. The only option was to finish the job. She would have to go back to London and repeat the mission, albeit with different arrangements.

The risk increased because there would now be a degree of alarm and suspicion raised, and the approach to the second assignment would need to be very different to avoid creating a visible crime footprint.

She also realized that any failure to comply placed her in immediate danger, whereas completing the assignment would yield the large sum shown on the copied Banker's draft.

She weighed her options and decided to continue. She thought briefly about the choice of vehicles for the rest of the journey. No-one knew she had left this car in these services; no-one knew she had planned this vehicle swap. It was safest to stay with the Peugeot and to continue the journey.

She picked up the cheap, garish Nokia phone from under the passenger seat of the Peugeot, held down the 2, which power dialled a number beginning +31. After six rings a phone operator style voicemail cut in. She listened to the standard greeting and said "Yes, one week." and then hung up.

Then she flipped the battery from the back of the cell-phone, prized out the SIM card and walked to a nearby refuse bin. She deposited the remnants of her apple and then walking back to the car dropped the SIM into a nearby kerb-side storm drain. As she approached the Peugeot, she stooped to look at the tyres, as if checking pressures. She was checking underneath for any signs of interference.

She re-entered the car, flicked the ignition and smiled to herself as the car started. A few moments of fiddling with the new sat-nav and she was ready to leave.

She pushed the defunct phone into the glove box and manoeuvred the car back onto the Autoroute, still heading South-East.

Broken in

"So, Jake, what other things and why do you think there's still danger?" asked Bigsy, "I think we, no you, should take all of this to the cops and get the professionals on to this. If you are really in danger, then they should have the best ways to help."

"Let me finish. I didn't think any of this was that important until right now," said Jake. "There's a difference between getting some sections together for a piece of low-key investigative journalism, compared with having one accidental death followed by a murder of a friend right on the doorstep."

Clare had finished transferring her list from the cereal packaging to a sheet to paper. It was the same list as the original scribble, but now, neatened and written starkly, it did seem to point towards a story.

Jake continued to explain the Collins interview to Clare and Bigsy.

"So the interview with Darren was supposed to be routine," he continued, "Successful fly-boy poser with big shiny wheels – except we are talking almost Formula One prices for this car – it does over 240 miles per hour, and there are only a few dozen variants in the world."

"But as the interview started, I could see that Collins looked rattled. It wasn't my questions or anything to do with the interview, but here we have a Mr Successful who had asked to be in our 'Flaunt' section now stuttering over his words and seeming to be very disengaged."

Clare and Bigsy exchanged a glance, "So you knew he was freaked about something; did you ask him about it?" asked Bigsy.

"Yes, I tried to," continued Jake, "but initially Collins dismissed it saying he'd got a big deal going down. Of course, I needed to ask him some background questions about his company and how he had made his money because it's not so apparent as a footballer hero or popstar. He gave me a "bit o' this and a bit o' that" type of line. My original assessment seemed right that he was a fly-boy."

Jake recounted this section of the interview. Collins had started in trading with perfumes and other market barrow-boy items. He'd moved into a small and legitimate import/export business and then seemed to strike it rich with a few large deals where he appeared as the middleman in large transactions. Jake wondered whether there was anything dubious, like drugs, along the way, but the basics seemed to be much more to do with conventional commercial intermediation.

"Yeah, he seemed to have a knack of making a turn on big trade deals between countries," continued Jake, "but I couldn't see anything illegal in the basic story.

"Apart from the dodgy perfumes when he started out. Hey, even the most august of today's rich and famous may have started pushing bootleg records or car aerials."

Bigsy nodded and thought of a couple of well-known British millionaires.

Jake continued, "But partway through the interview, Collins said something very unusual. I can't remember it exactly, but it was along the lines that with him being successful and all, he had to take certain precautions."

"That was the only part of the interview where he seemed fully engaged. I took this to be posturing like a lot of popstars have 'security' and bouncers and so-on. He said 'no' that there was more to it than that. He said that if ever anything were to happen to him, there was more than just financial insurance for him. That there was a special process - I took it to mean like a legal process - to handle his affairs. That's when he said something odd. He knew my machine was running and he said, "Yes I have a special code which can stop the process", and then he gave me a number- which at the time sounded like a phone number."

"I looked at him surprised that he had done this. He said it didn't mean anything to me anyway, so what was the harm in telling me. He did look, pointedly, at my machine when he said this though."

"I decided at this time to lighten up the conversation before we closed (tricks of the trade, always leave them feeling good), so I asked him some more questions about his car. It's a nutter, by the way, goes so fast that it is practically unusable on British roads. The acceleration is like a fast motorbike. It has these really cool doors, though, they sort of swing upwards."

Jake paused. He could see that Clare and Bigsy were taking in the main story and the piece about the car was an incidental distraction.

"And you know," said Jake, "I've got the recording of pretty much all of this - the Arabs, the argument, the American, and the interview with Darren Collins. It's back at my place - and not bad quality. My little gadget boosts the volume during the quiet pieces, you know.

"I didn't even get to listen to it again because the story got cut and then I had to go on that wild goose chase to Liverpool for the footballer story."

"So the next thing we need is the recording from Jake's," said Bigsy.

"Okay," said Clare, "but we need to think first – and that includes thinking about getting the police involved and also about safety".

"I agree, although at the moment, by pure chance, no one knows I'm here at Bigsy's," said Jake, "whereas they may expect me to show up at my flat, the Police station or my office. Call me a chicken, but it might be better for me to lay low until we've heard that tape again and then maybe to call the police when we have all of the evidence. I will want to be taken somewhere out of the way if things are as bad as they seem."

"I also think the only person who would know about me making the recording would be Collins – and I suppose other journos could work it out, but it's pretty unlikely that anyone is thinking about it."

"Yeah," said Bigsy, "And it's funny that we still all call it 'tape' when we all know its digital!" Clare and Jake both simultaneously turned as if to hit Bigsy, who was ready to defend himself with the frying pan.

Delays and findings

A few streets away, Jake's apartment had been watched for around two hours. Two local petty criminals sourced by a mysterious American were looking for the best way into the flat. The two burglars had seen a few people leave during early morning and then and some routine delivery of milk and mail, but the property looked easy enough to enter.

It was easy. A communal door to the stairwell. No special locks, no alarm, not even an entry camera.

Jake's door was easy to open. Inside it was easy to see why. There were not a lot of valuable items. There were books, CDs, a few magazines, a fancy plasma TV and a sleek MacBook laptop. The two intruders opened a large blue IKEA bag they had brought with them and dropped the MacBook into it. They riffled through the CDs, picking up a large pile of hand-labelled ones and added those to the collection.

Then they started a long and mainly silent and thorough search of the apartment, picking a few further items to add to their collection in the bag. They seized paper notepads, a few electronic gadgets, a couple of memory sticks, a digital camera and a music player. By now, they were using a second IKEA bag. Their search lasted less than ten minutes, and then they looked at one another, then at the rooms they had searched which still looked much as when they entered. They re-opened the door, left and one of them reset the lock such that their entry would not be obvious.

Struggling downstairs with the two bright blue bags, they slipped around the nearby street corner into a parked and slightly dented white van. Then a short drive of no more than a few hundred yards to meet the American again who had been patiently waiting for them in a nearby coffee shop. In a few moments the three of them were in the van and mingling with the London traffic.

On the French Autoroute, things had slowed to a standstill. There had been an accident ahead, and both lanes seemed blocked. Amelia looked into the air and saw a helicopter. Air ambulance. There was going to be a significant delay. She switched on the radio and tuned to a classics channel.

This gave her some time to reflect. Her best option was to get back to Cannes and then complete the alibi from the first assignment. She could also review the ease of access to the target, based upon the information and addresses given. Most of that could be done by the internet, but she would not use any communications until she returned to Cannes. She did not want any signals which could pinpoint her until she was good and ready.

She drank from the bottled water. It said 'sport water' on the side. She wondered what the difference was.

The delay outside Lyon became excruciating. The accident had pretty much closed the Autoroute. By the time Amelia was moving again, nearly two hours had passed. The French emergency services had been driving along the hard shoulder. By the position of the helicopter, it looked as if the accident was at least a couple of kilometres ahead. As she edged forward, most of whatever had happened had been cleared.

Off to the side of the road, like some felled dinosaur, was an articulated truck, on its side. As she drove past it, she knew the rules about not slowing to look, but it was almost unavoidable after two hours of boredom and then a chance to see the source of the inflicted pain.

As she started to pick up speed again, Amelia noticed that she had consumed more fuel than expected as a consequence of the holdup and would now need to stop somewhere again to fill up for the last part of the journey.

The American was in a Lebanese restaurant in London. He sat in a private room with the two men who had visited Jake's flat. Together they had been sifting through the contents of the blue bags, looking for something very specific.

The American picked up the digital recorder. "We need to check this," he said, "and also the computers." He flicked quickly through the menu on the Olympus. It showed dates and durations of recordings.

He scrolled the dates and located an entry around two weeks earlier when Jake had visited Darren Collins. The recorder showed a note "Uploaded Oct, 27". So, Jake had moved the recording to his PC.

They opened the Macbook; the screen had a big diagonal crack, but still immediately sprang to life and displayed a blue background with a small number of icons, including, to their surprise, a small picture of the digital recorder. A click later and they were in a folder full of voice recordings. A few moments later they were scrolling to the date of Jake's visit and a click later they listened to the recording, which began with a lengthy, if muffled conversation by the Arabs, followed by the interview with Darren Collins.

The whole recording was stuttery, which seemed to be a factor of the damage suffered to the computer, as if the disk was having trouble reading the file.

The American shook his head and thought, "I hate these Brit criminal low lives. They can wreck anything."

He weighed up the odds of finding anything else useful from the two criminals and then reached in his pocket to produce an

envelope counting a large number of banknotes. "It's all here",
he said, "you can count it later, but at the moment I need you
out of here. If you stay, you will be in danger and remember,
if you meet or see me again, you will also be in danger.
Goodbye"

He dismissed the two burglars, and they left the restaurant.
The American remained in the room for another hour. He had
loaded his own computer and linked it to the damaged one
stolen from Jake. He selected some specialised software,
copied the stuttering sound recording across to his computer,
spent some time editing it and then cut a copy of the modified
recording to a USB stick in his own PC.

Next, the American made a phone call, "I have something I
think you should hear," he said.

After a few minutes of discussion, the American assembled
Jake's belongings back into one of the blue bags. He placed his
own PC into a backpack and then, carrying both bags, he left
the room.

Safety First

"I agree with Bigsy," said Clare. "We need to think about safety – one of us needs to go back to Jake's, but," looking at Bigsy, "...it will better for it to be one of us two, Bigsy."

"...or both of us," answered Bigsy, "that way, we can look out for one another."

Clare shot a glance to Bigsy and then to Jake, "...or we could just call the police right now?" said Clare.

"The thing is...", said Jake, "... there's a little bit more".

They looked back at Jake. He looked sheepish.

"Well, after the calls from the American, I did call him back", said Jake,

"He asked to meet me and to explain a few things about the meeting with Darren. I asked him why, and he said there was a good story for me as well as some information for him. He said that I might be in some danger, but that I should not call the police. Also that all was not what it seemed when I saw him with the Arabs at Collin's office. I agreed on a date to meet him at 'Yo Sushi's' for lunch, - you know - the one across the bridge from Westminster. I thought he might have been a possible client, and that is why I let it run".

"Jake", sighed Clare, "Is there anything else you haven't told us?" she asked, "we can't help you if you don't tell us everything."

"Clare's right", said Bigsy, "This is looking quite dangerous, and I don't want to be finding out extra facts when it's just too late!"

"Okay," said Jake, "the only other thing is my meeting with the American is tomorrow!"

Clare looked at Jake and Bigsy," We can get a lot done today", she said.

"We can get the recording from Jake's, try to find out some more about Lucien's murder, make a list of everything we know and then decide whether we should take it to the police, even despite the American's warning to Jake."

"I also think Jake should stay here", said Clare, "If someone is looking for him, it would be stupid to return to his flat. Also, no-one will be able to connect the three of us. Jake, take my phone, switch yours off and don't answer any calls, except Bigsy's number. Once this is clearer, we can re-evaluate."

All three thought this sounded very melodramatic, although Lucien's murder meant they knew they were getting into something perilous.

Bigsy suggested that he and Clare travel over to Jake's. Bigsy already had a key to Jake's flat, which had sometimes been useful if they were meeting there in an evening and Jake was late - which was often the case. They decided to use taxis to get around. It wasn't far from Bigsy's to Jake's, but they could be invisible for longer in taxis.

"Jake," said Clare, "This is important. If you don't hear from us by phone in two hours, you must call the police anyway."

Jake nodded his acceptance and looked at his watch. By now, it was ten-thirty in the morning.

In France, the Peugeot was just pulling into the diesel line in the service station. Amelia driver got out and quickly filled the tank of the car. She paid with Euros and was back on the road inside ten minutes. Another three hundred kilometres to Cannes, mainly Autoroute.

Clare had a good idea on the way to Jake's. They would stop off at the nearby Tesco metro supermarket and buy a small quantity of groceries. Bigsy liked this because it could be a new supply of junk food.

Clare's point was to make it look as if they were routinely shopping and then carrying something into Jake's. If no-one was watching, it didn't matter if they were, it would look as if they were doing something normal. The carrier also gave them a container for their return journey. They splashed out on a £3.00 recyclable bag, which had robust handles and looked as if it could take some weight.

Getting into Jake's was easy enough, although they had both wanted to look around the area first. In reality, with no-one watching, the visit looked as if it would be uneventful.

Bigsy went straight to the kitchen and switched on the kettle while Clare looked around the fairly neat room for the recorder and Jake's MacBook. To begin with, neither of them considered anything abnormal in the flat. Then Clare noticed that Jake's computer was missing. And there were none of Jake's computer disks either.

"It looks as if Jake's computer has gone!" called Clare to Bigsy. He walked in and surveyed the room.

" Definitely," he said, looking at where the laptop was normally situated.   Then he looked under the desk, "The Wi-Fi connection is still here," he said, dropping into his professional techno-babble. He traced wires to another box, "and here's Jake's backup drive," he proclaimed, pulling a small dusty box from the floor behind the desk. "I installed this myself," he said," I knew Jake would be hopeless at this type of thing, so I set him up a little box to do the backups automatically overnight, as long as he left the computer switched on".

He carefully unplugged the box, which was about the size of a large novel and put it, with its connecting wires, into the Tesco's bag. Then he looked through a couple of other shelves and asked whether Clare had found the digital recorder. Clare shook her head. They continued to search through drawers. Bigsy found a stash of Mars chocolate bars and added them to the Tesco bag.

"Okay," said Bigsy, "Let's get out of here, we have everything useful". As they left, Bigsy texted to Jake that everything was okay.

Around a mile away, Trueman and Green were leaving the police station. They had spent most of last night and the morning together continuing the investigation. They were pretty sure that the identity information for Lucien Deschamps was accurate. They were also surmising that his background was legitimate, and they could not find links of him to anything even slightly off colour. No parking tickets, nothing.

"C'mon," said Trueman, realising they had worked a solid twenty hours, "a swift pint is in order."

They trooped over the road to the nearby pub. Inside were a brown bar and several roughly placed brown tables, with four chairs around each table. There were three men, each alone, sitting in the bar. A fruit machine twinkled lights in the corner and television without sound was running an old soccer match on a Sky TV channel.

They picked a corner table, and Andy Green ordered two pints of beer from the bar. "What do you make of it?" he asked as he sat down, balancing the beers on slightly curled beer mats on the dark brown table.

"It's all dead ends," answered Trueman, "A blame-free victim, no enemies, no suspicion of crime connections, yet a clinically executed assassination.

"The only woman suspect is captured on TV inside the gallery and across the road, yet the car with false plates she is being driven in seems to disappear without a trace in London's traffic. There are no traceable cell phones to give whereabouts, and no-one else has come forward with any comments. We can up the stakes with a poster appeal, but I wonder what this was all about."

Green nodded his agreement.

"It's as if this was the wrong victim, but there was hardly anyone else in the gallery. Those present have all got strong stories and nothing to create any reason for anything like this."

"So maybe it was the wrong victim..." ventured Green, "...I know we still need to run lots of checks, but the victim's basic story seems legitimate."

"Yeah, I was wondering too," responded Trueman.

"The gallery was open for Press viewings when this happened, not for the general public. Yet Deschamps was an office worker. I think this may be the lead - perhaps the murderer thought Deschamps was someone else."

They looked at one another. "So how did Spurs get on?" continued Green, sipping at his pint.

Ed Adams

Sunshine and shades

" The French Riviera;
a sunny place for shady people"

Postcard from Cannes

Cannes

Cannes was crowded with a trade event. The city famous for the film festival was used for much of the year for other less well-known events and had many ingredients for a good week away from the office for various types of commercial visitors. Whether it was TV soaps, physiology, retail technology or yachts, there was some show or convention and Cannes could provide lavish hotels and a great backdrop.

It was November, but the splendour of the Mediterranean resort was undiluted. Sun bleached, supersaturated colours and the unmistakable allure of a sheikh resort, even if it was only a week or so before it would plunge into Winter. The sky was bright blue, cloudless and a big contrast to a few days earlier when Amelia had left, and there had been a steady rain against a darkened sky. The elements were feeling playful in the last moments of the transition to the darker seasons.

She drove slowly along the Croisette, past the Palais de Congress where the film festival and many of the trade shows were held. She was heading back to the Carlton but had to lose the Peugeot first.

The Carlton was one of the most splendid hotels along the Croisette. A gaggle of valets and doormen stood outside. Amelia drove slowly past, then turned into a side street and sought a parking spot for the car close to the hotel.

For Amelia Brophy, this town was a perfect place to create an alibi. She could arrive, book into the trade conference in an obvious way and then use Nice airport as a hub during the week to move around to follow her instructions. She could easily disappear into the conference of several thousand people and at the end of the week would have perfect evidence of her whereabouts from badges, booking-in materials and the general paraphernalia of the conference.

She drove the Peugeot to a parking lot near to the train station and then walked back to the Carlton hotel, a few blocks away. By her planning, she had now ostensibly been in Cannes for three days. The conference was soon coming to its close. Her documentation and travel would be consistent with spending the week in Cannes.

There was no link with the events at the gallery or with the unusual route she had taken from the UK back to the conference. The change of orders had interfered with her original plan, but as a professional, she knew she needed to reach her anonymous bolthole in the Carlton and then to take stock of what to do next.

Her room at the Carlton was luxurious. She had not chosen a suite, which would be easier to notice if unused, but a room of the type that many conferences booked in large quantities. Unoccupied rooms overnight at a large conference were nothing unusual to the hotel staff, who had seen everything. As she walked back into her sea-facing room, she saw the jacket she had hung outside of the wardrobe, a PC laptop switched on with a screen saver and the bed already showing turn down service, complete with a little chocolate confection on both of the pillows. The whole room told a short story to any staff that happened to drop by.

She threw the envelope onto the bed and headed directly to the shower. Two days of travelling after an arduous job in London gave her a great sense of need to freshen up. She also transformed herself from businesswoman to a somewhat more sophisticated and continental look, wearing a casual blouse and a light-coloured jacket over black trousers and some sharply-pointed high-heeled shoes. If before she had looked the archetypal travelling businessman, she now looked far more 'Continental-European' and casual.

Then she sat down with her computer to start to consider her next actions. She began to look up information about Jake and the 'Street' magazine.

A business transaction

Bigsy and Clare travelled in a second taxi back to Bigsy's place. As they arrived, they noticed that one of Bigsy's flatmate's cars had managed to park close to the house, a rare feat in this part of Central London.

Rick worked for a well-known estate agents' chain, and they had given many of their mobile employees' cars that were all almost identical Minis. The vehicles were tricked out with a unique green, black and yellow camouflage paint job which also advertised the estate agency firm. They had become a frequent and commonplace sight on the streets of London. Inside, Rick was chatting affably to Jake, and they turned as Clare and Bigsy walked in.

"I was telling Rick about our plan to take a couple of days to photograph London for your project Clare," he lied, and both Bigsy and Clare picked up from this that Jake was saying nothing about what had been happening, to Rick.

"I told Rick we might need to do some detailed planning this evening". Rick smiled, "Yeah, that's great, I'm out tonight seeing a gig over in Camden. I may stay out over there".

The four continued to chat and then Rick made some excuses and prepared to leave for his evening.

"Okay, so what did you find?" asked Jake, in hushed tones. The others explained; Jake's flat looked superficially normal, but there had been a break-in, and the laptop, digital recorder and many CDs had gone.

"But look," Bigsy exclaimed, "this is your backup unit, and they didn't take it. Please tell me you are backing up your computers the way I told you?"

Jake smiled, he was known to be somewhat lackadaisical on most things related to technology, but because of his work, the one thing he was good at was backups. The infamous 'missing Royal College Report" had led to this fastidiousness for backup because he'd nearly lost his job when he deleted an important story, which had been partly written by somebody else from the office. He'd had to spend four or five days, including midnight hours, to get the work done again so that his colleague didn't suffer, although it also taught Jake to play it safe when using computers.

Half a world away, in Riyadh, Saudi Arabia, another scene was unfolding in this capital city grown from the desert. Riyadh's skyline is dominated by two enormous towers, one featuring a pointed building and the other taking the appearance of a crown. They are known as Al Faisaliah and the Kingdom Tower. The Faisaliah building's top area features a revolving restaurant, from where it is possible to look out from the capital to the city and the desert. The restaurant is shaped like a ball and has a distinctive and more private area for smoking exquisite cigars. The meeting was taking place in this restaurant.

In keeping with the dress code of Saudi Arabia, five of the six men seated around the table were wearing conventional Arab clothing, three with the traditional red and white chequered headdresses and the other two with the less common white. The sixth man was wearing a western suit, elegant but quite understated. White shirt and red tie of similar hue to the colours in the headscarves.

Ed Adams

They had been drinking fruit drinks and eating from a light tabbouleh and meze. Then one of the men spoke to the group, in English, of the situation they had convened to discuss.

"We will need to re-examine our trade clearance processes," he stated, "The route we have been using has been compromised - we will need to find another way. Mr Fredriksson here is to help us create the next route for our shipments. Mr Fredriksson, can you explain how this will work?"

Fredriksson was the suited westerner in this group. From Sweden, slim, blond hair, spectacles and a light tan suggesting someone well-travelled, he started his explanation. It was filled with business jargon but essentially said that he could facilitate the creation of some new trading processes which could help certain transfers of large sums of money on a global scale. These needed to go through 'special' procedures before the money was available for use.

To do what he intended, he needed some substantial down-payments from the assembled group. This was his fee for the work and separate from the further great operating expenses he expected to incur in creating the new environment.

The five Arabs switched into Arabic conversation for around ten minutes, and Fredriksson waited patiently. It was the second meeting; in the first one, there had been much bargaining to reach a position. He knew that when working with this group, he would need to build in some points which could be conceded as well as some individual handling fees payable to each of the people around the table.

"We will need to negotiate the detail of your terms, but we accept the general approach." The five Arabs nodded their acceptance and then continued to speak to one another in Arabic.

Fredriksson said, "In that case, gentlemen, I will bid you all good evening. I can catch the next flight to London at 0200 and this will mean I can start making the arrangements. Overall this is going to take around three weeks to set up. My colleague will be in contact to finalize the payment terms. Please understand this agreement is irreversible, and once we start, there will be no going back."

The five Arabs nodded "Shukran," said their leader "Ma'assalama!" Fredriksson stood, bowed his head slightly, made eye contact with each of the Arabs and then left the table and walked back towards the staircase from the cigar room, back to the express elevator and the ground floor.

Then a detour to his room on the 40th floor using a separate elevator where he collected an already packed slim traveller bag and then made his way again to the ground floor.

He walked across the front lobby where a combination of Arabs sipped tea in a conventional Arabic way, from tiny cups and Western-looking businesspeople sat in huddles talking about deals and business in the Kingdom. He noted the absence of women in this strict Islamic country.

The lobby entrance was vast sweeps of breath-taking glass, and as he approached, he signalled to the doorman, and within a few seconds, a sleek black Lincoln Town car had pulled up outside the lobby. He could head straight for the airport, out through the suburbs and across the desert to the vast Khalid International airport, with its massive underground car park, huge mosque and misleading architectural design like a major American hub. Deceptive because the airport lacked shops or other conventional Western trappings. He steeled himself for what he knew would not be a particularly pleasant wait for his plane.

A matter of procedure

Trueman and Green had no idea of the magnitude of the situation they were entering. They knew the killing of Deschamps was professional, had worked out that it was probably mistaken identity, had seen a woman on camera leaving the crime scene but had no further idea about who could have been involved.

As procedure, they were following up on the invitations to the gallery show and discovered that the invitation list for the preview day was short and included mainly trade and some magazine and news journalists.

The trail had led them to the Street magazine and Jake's editor, Robert Davis. He was not particularly phased to have a couple of policemen invite themselves to his offices, as from time to time the magazine got itself caught up in the periphery of other investigations. The nature of their journalism meant they would stumble into mostly petty matters and so there would be an occasional visit as part of routine procedures.

This time, the discussion was about the new showing by a subversive and controversial artist who had been exhibiting near Sloane Square. The show start was delayed because of a murder, played down in most press coverage.

"Mr Davis," began Trueman, "We have a few questions about one of your journalists."

"Fire away," answered Davis, "But remember I may have to take advice on certain questions". Robert Davis was slightly intrigued by the turn of events and realized that Jake had been at the show. Trueman explained the background and Davis responded.

"Well, the whole story was put on hold after the death and the delay to the opening. We keep our stories upbeat unless we are targeting a celebrity, but this situation of a 'murder in the gallery' didn't fit with the monthly flow of the magazine.

"We can't beat the newspapers to the punch on topicality and, frankly, the delayed show pushes it further back in the magazine. We may do a more general piece later, but at the moment there's a couple of other stories we pushed up as we bumped this one down."

As he said it, Davis realized that there were now three stories by Jake which hadn't been delivered over the last few weeks; moreover, Jake was now sick from work.

In a light-hearted way, Davis recounted to the police, firstly Jake's Liverpool fiasco with the substantial expenses but no story, then the current art exhibition and finally the collapse of part of the "fast boys" story because of the accidental death of Darren Collins.

Green and Trueman looked at one another. This was a

promising lead. Here was someone supposed to be at the art show, someone with a recent track record of absences and on the periphery of two recent deaths.

Davis went on to point out that Jake may be erratic but was a good writer and had been with the magazine for at least eighteen months. These situations were close together, but frankly, in the business of 'Street', errant journalists were not a particularly unusual occurrence.

They walked back into the busy bus-filled street by the magazine's offices. "We're on to something," said Trueman, "Mr Jake Lambers is about to get a visit."

Back at Bigsy's flat, Bigsy was now intent on fiddling with computers, wires and the backup unit from Jake's place, Clare and Jake chatted idly, but waited expectantly for the little box to burst into life.

"Eureka!" called Bigsy, "we have contact! Houston, the lights are now flashing!" and sure enough Bigsy had connected the backup box to one of his computers and now had access to the folder structure to read the files.

He browsed through the files, "Well done, mate - you followed the backup routine!" he said absently, to Jake as he looked at what was on the disk.

"We seem to have a good backup of your laptop." He scrolled along until he found the digital recorder directory and there inside it was a large selection of files containing recordings from various interviews conducted by Jake. And amongst them, was a recording from the date of Jake's meeting with Collins.

Bigsy clicked it. iTunes popped up on the computer, the software usually used to play music tracks, and then almost immediately, the sounds of the muffled meeting with the Arabs, interspersed with louder sounds of Jake drinking coffee.

"We can improve the sound quality a bit," said Bigsy, "But let's just listen to it through once". He fiddled around in his pocket whilst he said this and withdrew his keyring. "I'm also making another copy," he announced, showing a small electronic gizmo on his keyring, with a plug on its end to connect into the side of the computer.

He plugged the memory stick into the side of the computer and copied the still playing file into his storage device.

The recording ran for about five minutes with the muffled conversation, which was about something about trade routes and seemed to be quite agitated by the end.

There was then the distant conversation where Jake had met the group outside the room and then the click as the session finished, almost immediately running into a new session comprising Jake and Darren Collins sitting together in the place where the recorder was situated.

What followed was the interview Jake had described. There was nothing particularly interesting beyond the points which Jake had accurately recounted to Bigsy and Clare, but both Bigsy and Clare picked up on the agitation in the tone of Collin's replies.

It was as if Collins didn't want to be there doing the interview but was still trying to give polite replies to the questions he was being asked. As Jake had said, there was also the section where he talked about the secure code and gave a number which all three of them wrote down. It was "Blue Flame mph 7539".

After twenty-five minutes or so, the interview concluded, and then the recording stopped abruptly. There was a moment of silence in the room.

"See..." said Jake, "...I was pretty accurate with what I told you." The others nodded agreement.

"We need to get a better version of the first section," said Bigsy, "I'm sure I'll have something to help this."

He fiddled around with the computer again for another ten minutes.

"OK," he said, "I've added some sound mixing software to this PC. It's only a trial edition from a download, but we get to use it for thirty days!"

Clare and Jake looked at one another; they were hardly leading-edge counter-espionage agents if they were using free trial software to crack hidden messages. To their joint amazement, the program started up, and after a few screens of text imploring them to buy the full version, it eventually led them to a complicated control panel.

"Drag and drop," said Bigsy, by this time in full geek-ville. He found the folder with Jake's recording and dropped the little file icon into the new program. Some wiggly lines appeared which looked like the sound wave of the recording. Bigsy pressed 'play', and the same bad recording started again; only now he could change the sound quality. To begin with, he was playing with controls akin to the tone controls on a hi-fi, but then he started clicking other buttons, and to the surprise of Jake and Clare, the sound started to get clearer and the background hum and other interference sounds seemed to melt into the background.

"I'm using a multi compressor to sweep for the best frequencies," mumbled Bigsy, "and set a shelf for the low end to cut out that low rumble".

"Whatever it is, it's a bloody genius," chuckled Jake, amused at Bigsy's intensity in this exercise. Bigsy saved the settings and rewound the recording to the start.

"Let's listen," he said.

PART TWO

Ed Adams

Puzzle Palaces

"The best secrets are the most twisted"
— Sara Shepard, Twisted

Langley

The National Security Administration in Langley, Virginia, USA is set inside a complex often referred to as Fort Meade.

To locals, there is another nickname, "the Puzzle Palace" because it is used as the most extensive electronic surveillance and counter-espionage environment on the planet.

This means that Langley eavesdrops. It has giant computers able to monitor millions of phone calls and e-mails each day. Most items tracked are innocent. Langley has to be good at spotting the few that are not.

At that moment, a particular chain of events was beginning to raise a few alerts in their systems. There was activity in Saudi Arabia as several seriously wealthy Arabian businessmen were clustered together with a person who the NSA had been monitoring for some time.

They had been particularly clever at triangulating the individual under surveillance. He was skilled at counter-espionage technique and often used multiple cellular phones in a way that made him difficult to track. His smart part was that he also kept a routine phone which he regularly used, which could create a decoy usage print of normal behaviour. The not so smart part was that he used different phones but often first enabled them from either his home or his office. This gave a useful signal to the monitoring authorities, who could then pick up the cell phone number and the handset serial number, by noting its first activation from a known location. After that, it was easy enough to switch on tracker software to record any use of the phone.

So the person being tracked, JA/RU/059 was easy to follow, and the monitoring of his meeting with the Arabs in Riyadh had been a matter of identifying his cell phone and noting five other long usage cell phones all in the same location.

Langley had noted another 657 phones in the same location as the person they were monitoring. They had quickly reduced it to 47 phones with similar arrival and departure times. The monitoring picked up usage consistent with a meeting. The group all arrived within a few minutes of one another, they all left and split up at roughly the same time. The central mark had left around 35 minutes earlier and next been stationary at Riyadh's airport, before the signal had de-activated. Since that time there was no signal anywhere.

NSA removed several people from their remaining list as highly improbable, but finally identified a small group within the cell phones left, that were high profile individuals.

NSA also cross-checked their findings with their "Five Eyes" allies. This included the UK's GCHQ, although the British did not have the same level of monitoring capability as the Americans.

The theory was that their suspect had met around five senior Arabian businessmen in Riyadh. They had been in a high-profile location, spent an hour together, and then dispersed. Their suspect had travelled to Riyadh's airport, de-activated his phone and was now no-longer visible, The NSA were now tracking the routine phone of the suspect, for its re-activation, but so far there had been no signal.

The request for information from the Americans to GCHQ had also created an alert which had routinely also been passed to the UK's National Crime Squad, who normally worked in areas related to organized crime.

On this occasion, the alert was considered to be civil and consequently more relevant to the police forces than the counter-espionage units, with whom GCHQ regularly operated.

GCHQ passed the report to the National Crime Squad, who triaged the reported incident to decide whether to take action. Frugality ruled, and an economical low-key monitoring option was selected, partly as a consequence of the lowered terror threat level in the UK.

Sound reasoning

Fredriksson's plane from Riyadh was on time. The journey was about five and a half hours according to the schedule, but he also knew that early morning landings at London's Heathrow could be delayed. In the event, his arrival was punctual, and because he had been seated at the front of the plane, he'd taken full advantage of the available bed. He would also freshen up in the arrivals lounge allocated for the more privileged passengers of British Airways.

His objective now was to get into central London and to meet the American who had some interesting news. The American's name was Chuck Manners, which sounded part British and was a rather apt name for someone in his line of business. Chuck didn't seem to see the irony of his name, and it wasn't something to make a direct joke about. But Fredriksson normally thought of him as 'The American' in any case.

From Heathrow, he picked a taxi from the line and asked for Edgware Road, on the western outskirts of central London. Every taxi driver would know this location and the ride was around fifty minutes. Sure enough, the taxi pulled up at the appropriate office block, in an area which seemed to have a fair smattering of Arabic shops in the neighbourhood. He stepped out of the cab, walked the few steps to the office block, pressed a buzzer and was admitted to the lobby area and the elevators where the American had his office.

A few miles away, in Bigsy's flat, Bigsy's technical attempts to adjust the sound from the recording were surprisingly successful. The first part of the recording comprised the majority of the conversation which had taken place in the next room, interspersed with some loud sounds of Jake stirring and sipping coffee.

The dialogue started without much by way of introductions. This could be simply that the recording started a little way into the conversation. A softly spoken Arab with a definite edge to his accent, particularly on words with 'R' in them, had been describing the current transfer arrangements of some funds.

He explained the purpose of the arrangement with Collins to move funds efficiently and with the minimum of interest from other organizations. The recent development seemed to be that since 'they' (he did not say who) had become interested, it was slowing down the process to an unacceptable degree.

Bigsy, Clare and Jake assumed 'They' referred to the authorities in some form, whether police or some kind of regulatory organization.

The softly spoken Arab had continued explaining that the consortium that he represented was most displeased at the recent delays and irregularities in handling payments and that they were reviewing their options.

A second and gruff-sounding Arab took over, saying that the agreement between Collins and the consortium was ended because of recent developments. He wanted to know from Collins whether the current funds in transit would be rapidly processed. Then, the entire consortium may wish to seek a new business partner. The first Arab had continued saying that they needed to see an up-to-date list of the transactions still in progress and their anticipated completion dates.

Collins had blustered at this point. He had sounded

uncomfortable throughout the entire conversation and now was trying to explain the current position. The funds still involved seemed high, but Collins did not seem to have a clear idea of when the payments would all be complete. There was a pause, the gruff Arab then continued stating, in a very firm voice, that because of that uncertainty, the consortium would be invoking a clause in their original agreement to take back control of the remaining transactions.

The fees due to Collins would be revoked, and Collins would need to sign over control of the remaining processes to another one of their business associates. There was a noise of clicking and sounds of paper rustling. Collins was saying over the top of this that he was sure the situation could be fixed and that any action on the part of the consortium was premature.

"I disagree," said a new voice, well educated and to an English ear, it sounded rounded in a public-school kind of way. It must have been the third Arabian looking gentleman because the American had a clear southern state drawl when Jake had spoken to him later.

The voice continued, "We have followed the procedure in the original agreement. The basis of the agreement was clear when we started. You have given your word that you would handle this impeccably. We now have a difficult situation for the consortium and need your full co-operation. I strongly advise you to listen to my business associates and to follow their advice".

There was a long silence.

The first Arab, with a quiet voice, spoke again. "It will be much easier for all of us if we simply follow the original agreement. We need you to sign the document in the places indicated. We can take over from there and leave any finalization details to our other colleague, Mr. Manners."

The American spoke, for the first time since the recording had started, "Mr. Collins, I strongly urge you to take the advice of your business partners. I believe their legal agreement is binding and that they also have a solid point about the current status of our business transactions. Please do not make things more difficult through senseless obstinacy."

There was another pause. Collins asked if there was an opportunity for him to seek legal advice. He was told that the agreement was signed with full knowledge of what would happen in a situation of dispute. They reiterated that this situation was beyond contradiction.

There were a few more pauses and then Collins could be heard rather unenthusiastically agreeing to the demands of the group. Some rustling and scraping sounds, presumably of the paperwork being signed and then within a few moments, the sound of chairs moved around.

"A good decision," said the original softly spoken Arabic voice as the sounds turned to those of opening the office door and of people moving into the lobby area. Jake could then hear himself first making contact with the group and the clumsy exchange followed by the more strident exchange from the American asking to swap business cards.

The next section transitioned into the arrival of Collins in Jake's meeting room and the clear transcript, including the little sequence with the exchange of the number, but nothing else particularly noteworthy to the listeners.

There was a pause as Bigsy, Jake and Clare looked at one another at the end of the recording. They were all caught in thought and in particular of the tense discussion between the Arabs and Collins, which Jake was hearing for the first time.

Jake spoke first. "Well that puts a lot more of what has been happening into perspective," he commented, and the others nodded. "We still don't know exactly what the business is about, but it's clear that Collins has delayed some payments and the Arabs were not very happy. It sounds as if he has signed some rights over to the Arabs as part of this transaction."

Clare commented next, "It looks as if the Arabs were threatening him as well – we can't tell what the body language of the session was like, but the words certainly sounded menacing."

"And that is consistent with the look as they all left and with the way that Collins seemed shaken up when I was interviewing him," said Jake.

"And what about the American?" asked Bigsy. "He seemed to be there as some sort of heavy artillery if Collins got out of order!" he suggested.

"Okay," said Clare. "What about the code that Collins gave you. Was it a pass-code, an email login, a combination or what?"

They all stared at the code individually.

"Okay," said Bigsy, "but let's think about this first. If it is a password or code, we don't want it to be traced back to here that we are so that we are accessing from a place that someone could locate. And maybe we should try some internet searches first, in any case?"

"Good point!" echoed Clare, "We need to find a place with lots of people if we are going to try that."

Once again, they decided that Clare and Bigsy would make the journey, but before that, they decided to write out as many options for the code that they could invent, to try out which would work. They all felt they were getting somewhat paranoid but didn't want to take any chances after what had happened to Lucien and Collins.

For the record

In Edgware Road, Fredriksson had found the American's office quickly and approached the person seated at a solitary desk. It was Mr Manners, with his Southern drawl.

"Thank you for seeing me here," began Manners.
"Let's keep this to the point," responded Fredriksson.

"I've got the recording," Manners began, "and there is an important part for you. I've edited the important piece onto a short extract, which is on this memory stick."

He flipped the stick into a small player on the desk in front of him. There was a part of the conversation between Jake and Collins. They were talking about car prices and the McLaren supercar. Then Collins started to talk about the code and sure enough, gave information which seemed to confuse Jake.

Then the conversation moved on to a few other points finishing with the section about the arrangements for the photography session.

At the end, the American handed the stick to Fredriksson.

"Here you are," he said, "I think you can understand why I

have kept the original version as a type of insurance. You will do whatever you need to with this recording; yes, all of it is here, but I will be keeping the original and a paper transcript in a safe place."

Fredriksson nodded. The two men professionally understood one another. Each needed some leverage to be sure that there could be some trust and security between one another.

"There may be some sudden endings, but I doubt that you and I will ever meet again," said Fredriksson. They nodded to one another and Fredriksson left the office with the CD.

A few moments later, the American picked up the CD player and walked out of the office. He didn't look back. He would never need to see this office again. Its use for 48 hours had been all he needed.

Bigsy and Clare were also working on the meaning of the recording. They had heard the whole scene involving the Arabs and had a pretty clear idea that it was a threat and that Collins was coerced into something before his death. They also had the code number and suspected it to be a telephone number.

"Okay," said Jake as Clare and Bigsy made their way to the door. Outside they hailed another taxi for the short ride to Regent's Street.

In Cannes, France, the phone rang in the Amelia's hotel room. She paused. No-one knew she was here. She answered it cautiously. "Hello?" she said, giving away as little information as possible.

"Ms Brophy, I trust you are refreshed from the conference?" came a clear voice, "We have some interesting opportunities to discuss; I believe you saw the paperwork earlier? It would be advantageous for us both to meet at, let's say, 4 p.m. at the Martinez. I am in room 731. Please do come straight to the room. This is quite important."

The phone clicked off.

Amelia Brophy scribbled down the room number 731. He knew the Martinez, which was another famous hotel along the Croisette. She looked at her watch. It was already three twenty-five in the afternoon. A ten-minute walk to the other hotel. Was this a trap?

Lots of people knew she was in Cannes from the perspective of her alibi. She had been careful to separate her undercover role from the obvious story she had been creating. She was sure that the call was from the clandestine side of what she had been doing, and it was from someone very close. It had to be related to the people who had given her the envelope with the unexpected contents.

She ran some scenarios in her head. Meet, Fight, Flight. She decided that she should visit but would take some defensive precautions. Still logged on to her computer, she loaded her email software, selected scheduled email, created a short message and pressed enter. The email would not leave her system immediately. It was held in a 'pending' file until 17:30.

If she returned, she would cancel the message.

If there were a problem, the message would go to an interesting area in eBay, where it would form part of an auction. The auction was somewhat specialized and should not attract unwanted attention. This process had become a way to build insurance for some rather unconventional associates to operate together anonymously.

Placing advertisements for an obscure category of heavy equipment, they were able to post contracts about people they wanted removed. It allowed bidders to use the site anonymously to publish contracts and then bid to complete them.

The only use was for professional assassin contractors who

considered themselves in danger. Respondents were also in the same line of business and operating on a strict bounty basis.

She left the computer switched on but emptied everything else from the room into a small holdall.

She placed the holdall in a cupboard in the room, which now looked unoccupied, except for the small laptop connected to the internet and a mains supply.

"Primed," she thought as she closed the door on her way out of the room.

Crazy

Here's to the crazy ones.
The misfits. The rebels. The troublemakers.
The round pegs in the square holes.
The ones who see things differently.
They're not fond of rules.
And they have no respect for the status quo.
You can quote them, disagree with them, glorify or vilify
them.
About the only thing you can't do is ignore them.
Because they change things.
They push the human race forward.
And while some may see them as the crazy ones, we see
genius.
Because the people who are crazy enough to think they can
change the world, are the ones who do.

--Steve Job

An apple a day

The main reason that Bigsy and Clare had selected to go to the Apple Store in Regent's Street was for anonymity. It was close by, had plenty of computers connected to the internet and a very fast-changing series of customers. By selecting a random computer (after some wait to be able to obtain one from the many students reading and sending emails) and then by using Google, they could quickly find out whether Bigsy's idea was correct.

Once more, they typed in the internet web search for the 'Blue Flame mph 7539' passcode sequence. They soon found a few Blue Flame websites and even several where the code number was also used. Bigsy flicked through the sites. One looked promising with 'Blue Flame' across the top and then a series of pictures of various engineering elements.

Bigsy clicked a few of the photographs and many words on the page, but nothing happened. "This doesn't lead anywhere," he said, "It's a dead-end - there has to be more," he continued. He flicked back to a couple of other sites. There has to be more than this list of gas fitters.

Clare looked the screen, "Wait," she said, "Blue Flame – a very fast car! – miles per hour!" She pointed to a Wikipedia entry.

Bigsy nodded, "Yes, good idea, there's a tie-in to Darren's interest in cars."

"Let's try it," said Clare, "and we should also write it down."

She reached into her jacket and found a flyer handed to her in the street.

Bigsy was looking through the entry. "Here we are," he said, "Blue Flame, a rocket car. Check this; It's the speed of the car. It is written to look like the start of a phone number. 622.407 – let's add the 7539 to the end."

Clare wrote the "phone number" on her paper and Bigsy clicked another search term. The screen flicked to another web page very different from the first one.

A picture of an apartment block, in Switzerland, with an address. It looked like an advertisement for rental, but also included a caption, which said "Suite 009 available for rental, reference Blue/FLA/me"

Clare and Bigsy re-read this. It was a reasonably unambiguous instruction to visit a specific town and a particular room.

"No way," said Clare, "This is too crazy." Bigsy nodded and continued to click on the keyboard. He was running a search for the city and apartments, to validate that this was a real address.

Sure enough, a Google map blinked back at them, and then a satellite image of the street, close to the lake.

He found that there were 89 rooms in the development, including nine suites. Clare continued to take notes as they flicked through the various websites. Bigsy looked to see if there was a way to find out about the specific suite referred to on the other web page. There was nothing.

For another 45 minutes, Bigsy ran other searches in an attempt to find a way to make useful contact with the apartments without a visit. There was nothing. They would need to visit in person to follow the instructions.

"Yay!" said Clare, "but this is starting to get expensive".

Canned Heat

The frontage of the Martinez was more understated than some of the other grand hotels along the front in Cannes. An original art deco confection, it had been substantially modernised over the last years, which meant it was well-equipped with the latest high-speed internet connections and extensive access to most of the world's cable TV.

Amelia walked across the sleek lobby, requesting a room and stipulating the sixth floor. As it was the last day of the conference, she knew there would be likely spare capacity, and she was rewarded with a room immediately.

She looked around for the elevators. She was used to looking as if she knew where she was going in hotels, while simultaneously scoping them out.

She noted the offices behind the reception area and that the reception was in a type of cul-de-sac area in the hotel. In a shootout, the area would be difficult to manage unless using the back exit by the side of the administration offices.

The elevator was also small inside, and as she pressed the button for the seventh floor, she noted that it didn't light, although the elevator did start to move. "Security," she thought, "someone going to floor seven isn't going to be noticed by travellers to other floors."

She wondered if this was accidental but recognised it as a typical security trick used by several Agencies as well as the Russian mafia. It also gave a signal to those in the know about the way a floor may not be quite what it seemed.

She glanced around the elevator for a camera, but there was nothing visible. Given the unlit button, she assumed that the elevator was wired, but that it would be exceptionally discreet.

Then to the floor. She exited the elevator and looked immediately to the rather grandiose and sweeping stairway. She looked over the edge making quick mental calculations about angles of view. She then walked down a floor to check the positions of exits and routes.

She sought her sixth-floor room and entered it using the swipe key. A good room, looking better than the standard room she had at the Carlton. A view of the sparkling sea. She walked to the bed, not turned down. She pulled down the bedcovers and pushed the courtesy cushions into the bed, making a form which looked like a sleeping body. She added the courtesy bathrobe to the ensemble and found the pillows (no doubt to be used by the turndown service) in a wardrobe. Now she drew the curtains, so the room was now dark. Going back to the door, she looked towards the bed. From the door, it gave every impression of a sleeping person, facing away from the door on the far side of the bed.

These preparations completed, she flipped the room card into her jacket pocket and made her way back to the stairway.

Now it was around ten minutes to four o'clock. She ascended to the seventh floor. "Givenchy Spa" said the signage.

The floor had almost no room markings. It was a well-thought-out plan for the most exclusive part of the hotel. If you didn't know where you were going, it was hard to find anything.

Amelia followed the signs towards the spa and along the way were several doors on the right-hand side. Each led to an entrance lobby. She looked in the first. Then she spotted the small door numbers discreetly placed by the bell push. She needed to go further to the end of the corridor.

At around five minutes to four, she was outside the requisite room, which had a public space lobby almost the size of the room she had left at the Carlton.

Amelia looked back along the corridor. Then she walked to the door, which had a small spy hole. It was blanked from inside. There was another adjacent door, which looked like service cupboards. If anything bad was going to happen, this was a tight spot to handle, and her best space management techniques didn't give her a good feeling. She thought back to the PC with its primed death contract in the other hotel.

Then she rang the bell of room 731.

Leaving the Apple Store and feeling triumphant, Bigsy and Clare used another black cab to get back to Bigsy's place. They had found the essential information they needed and had done it in an almost untraceable way.

Someone would need to visit the Apple store and get the security footage even to be able to spot them. Bigsy has also deleted the 'History' from the browsing they had just completed. It would not fool an expert but would at least slow someone down. They had also moved three times to different computers during their investigation, which also covered their tracks, along with the substantial other traffic of random shoppers, students and tourists into the store.

Back at Bigsy's, they told Jake what they had discovered and the linkage across to Zurich.

"So, Jake, what are we going to do next?" asked Clare "If we continue to look into this ourselves, then it is dangerous AND expensive!"

"I agree," replied Jake, "We're onto something, that's for sure. I think I'm in danger anyway, and I doubt the police will be able to stop that, short of hiding me somewhere. At the moment, this is a good place, because no one expects me to be here and we arrived here in a random way. I want us to try to link with the American, who has told me that I need to contact him. In any case. I know I'm asking you two to do a lot of this, but how about we make contact with the American tomorrow and then decide what to do next?"

"How much danger is there to meet the American?" queried Bigsy, "by your own account, he looked like a military-grade person."

"We need to think this through," replied Jake. Clare nodded.

Jake explained the arrangements for the next day. He was supposed to meet the American in 'Yo, Sushi,' a busy lunchtime restaurant chain just over the River Thames from Westminster. The location was also very close to Waterloo train station. They started to assemble a plan.

Bigsy would meet the American. Jake would be in the vicinity, in case it was essential, but they would keep him away from the American if practical.

Clare would control events by cell phone. They also needed an extra phone because they could not use Jake's. Clare must buy a cheap 'pay as you go' phone from a local store.

It would be suitably anonymous and meant that the three of them could communicate during the meeting. Jake knew the restaurant's location well and also that there was plenty of good viewpoints nearby all within a short walk of the famous landmark of the London Eye.

They contrived a plan. Privately, each realised they were dealing with professionals, and just hoped that their amateur efforts would be so far outside the way a professional would think that they would be able to make it work.

In Chelsea Police Station, Detective Inspector Trueman was still engrossed in the case. Although his other workload was heavy, this case had created some interesting developments.

He received information via a regular bulletin that a serious crime suspect with international connections had recently been tracked via the US National Security Administration. This person of interest had shown up first in Riyadh and then in London. They were now staying close to the area of the gallery and the murder.

Whilst this was probably co-incidence, the appearance of a serious 'player' on his patch was an interesting development. However, the timings of his arrival did not match the murder and Trueman viewed it as 'one to watch' rather than for direct enquiry.

Trueman was, however, interested in what had happened to Jake Lambers, the person who appeared to have given the tickets to Lucien Deschamps. After trying to contact Jake, at home, at his office and by phone, they were drawing a blank.

Jake's employers had admitted that Jake was something of a free spirit, but it was interesting that he didn't seem to have any visibility at all at the moment.

Trueman had some theories; maybe Jake was 'loose' somewhere; perhaps Jake was hiding for a reason yet to be determined or perhaps Jake was in trouble or worse.

Trueman had discussed this with Green, and they were examining places where Jake could have gone, including the pursuit of other stories. Green had obtained his cellular phone number from 'Street' and had contacted Vodafone to check for recent calls. There had been none since shortly after the murder of Lucien, and this was very much at odds with Jake's usually frequent usage pattern.

So, although it was not a very strong lead, Trueman and Green were trying to find Jake Lambers.

Dare

Fortune sides with they who dare.

–Virgil

Meet the Russians

At the Martinez, Amelia waited for the doorbell of room 731 to be answered. Apart from the entrance lobby, there was no particular clue to the type of place she was about to enter. As the door opened, she walked into a huge apartment. This may be a hotel room, but it was achingly expensive. The person opening the door was a tall, dark-suited blond-haired woman. "Please stand here, Ms Brophy," she said gesturing to a large area just inside the room.

The area contained a conference table for around six people and a set of doors leading out onto a sun-lit balcony. The curtains in the window fluttered lightly indicating the doors were already open. The room was chilled from an air conditioning set low. Two men stood up from their comfortable chairs further into the room. One wore a dark suit, white shirt and dark tie, the other a black leather three quarter length jacket.

"We need to ensure you are not carrying any form of weapon, or any form of listening device," said the woman. Her accent was strong, and her voice quite low. It reminded Amelia of a Russian accent, but she could not be sure.

The leather-jacketed man spoke. "I will be using an electronic sweeper to check you," he said. He reached to an aluminium case and retrieved a large electrically operated device with a large flat surface about half the size of a sheet of A4 paper. He clicked the device on saying, "If you are not carrying weapons or surveillance, then you have nothing to fear."

Amelia was used to this type of reception and knew they would not find anything because she had considered it too dangerous to carry anything to this group. He also noted the Russian's technique for searching and sweeping her and realised that this was effective looking but ultimately unsophisticated security. She mentally scored the man's technique and considered him to have professional training for his role, but not to a very high standard.

"Well, Ms Brophy," said the second man, wearing the elegant suit. He had a stronger Russian accent, typical of the inhabitants of Moscow, "we have someone you should meet."

The woman opened another door at the far end of the long apartment. The room was in three major sections. They comprised a meeting area, a sitting area and then an office area.

Alone, this was three or four times the size of the room Amelia had used in the Carlton. A flat screen television was switched on with no sound in the comfortable seating area. A program in Russian was playing, which looked like a news report. At the far end of the room another set of curtains billowed. There was another set of doors onto a balcony. The woman gestured to him to go on to the balcony. It was a large decked area, easily big enough for a reasonable sized party. A large oval wooden table was in front of him, big enough to seat six or eight people.

At the table sat a deeply tanned man in his mid-forties. He was wearing an open-necked shirt, and Amelia could see the glint of a heavy golden chain around his neck.

"Ah, Ms Brophy," he started, "It is very unusual to meet employees of your type. But then, it is unusual for these type of employees to need to do the same job twice. I think we both understand one another?"

Amelia nodded. She didn't want to get more drawn into the discussion than necessary. There were sometimes reasons to remain ignorant of certain situations. She knew the balcony was exposed. She was seven floors above ground, in a corner of the hotel. From the corner of her eye he could see the large white roof lettering spelling 'Martinez'. The penthouse complex she was in was under the last few letters of the huge sign.

"So, Ms Brophy, we have decided to give you the chance to complete the original job. I believe you will have seen the papers, which give more comprehensive information about our target. Please make sure you complete the assignment this time. And now look up behind you..."

Amelia looked up in the air again, back towards the sign. She noticed something on the 'Z'. it was a point of red light. The tanned man raised an arm. The red dot of light started to move slowly along the outline of the 'Z' and then down the building. It then traced a path towards her and finished on the middle of her chest. She knew it was a laser sight and she recognised it was on a high-performance weapon a long way away. She realised it was on a yacht either in the expanse of Mediterranean bay before him, or else in the harbour across to the left looking out from the hotel balcony. It appeared to be stabilised too, so from expensive kit, or with a cool hired hand.

"I see you have noticed my little exhibition," said the tanned man. "I know you know what this is. Today I am simply making a point. In a week, if I don't see the conclusion of our project, then the point I make may be somewhat sharper. We do understand one another?"

Amelia understood only too well. She had walked into a Russian crime syndicate, and they were now asking her to complete her assignment to kill Jake Lambers, or else she would be killed after a further week. The fact that the Russians has found her so easily suggested that even with her skill at becoming invisible, it was implausible to believe that she could stay hidden from this Russian group.

"I understand, and already have researched a repeat visit," she replied.

"Well then, let me bid you a good evening.," responded the Russian. "Cannes is remarkably pretty for this time of year; the sunset will be very soon, across behind those hills. In the last few moments as the light turns to evening, it is something spectacular to see," continued the Russian.

"I shall look at the sun setting on my way back to my hotel," responded Amelia, as she made her way towards the door to the penthouse. As she stepped back from the balcony decking, she noticed the way through to yet another area of the apartment and via a gate to a balcony garden where two tanned, streamlined women were sitting in what appeared to be a hot tub. This was certainly opulent and costing thousands of dollars per evening.

She nodded to the two men and then briefly met the eyes of the woman as he walked back to the exit from the room. She pointedly walked back to the stairs and then down the single flight back to the sixth floor, directly to her room. She opened the door theatrically and closed it again, still outside of the room, then slipping quickly around a corner and on towards another set of service elevators.

She had no idea whether anyone would be fooled that she had gone into the room, but he thought it would add some confusion if she was being followed. In addition, she now found a back way out of the hotel via the service elevator. She had noted that the penthouse gave a perfect view of the hotel entrance, filled with expensive cars. By not visibly leaving, it would give the Russians something to think about and for them to inevitably investigate her apparent lodging at this hotel.

She removed the jacket she had been wearing as she walked and dropped it into a roadside bin. She made her way back to the Rue d'Antibes, which is the main shopping thoroughfare in Cannes. As she approached the first Department store, she selected a new mountain gear style outer coat and an oversized check shirt. She also picked some miniature binoculars and a few other camping accessories, along with a black backpack. Ten minutes later, she was back on the Rue d'Antibes, walking towards the Carlton, wearing the new outer garment and carrying the backpack.

As with the Martinez, she was able to find a non-public way back into the Carlton, this time through a side door which led towards the kitchens. The door was propped open and looked as if it was a way for hotel employees to get outside to smoke during working hours. She followed the corridor inside, which had rubber bumpers along it, presumably because it was used to take large containers out to be picked up by trucks.

She gently clicked through a sprung door and found himself back in an area of high decoration and with ornate pictures on the wall. It was clearly part of a conference and meeting area of the hotel. She traced through this area and found herself back in the main bar area, then through a lobby to the main elevator and back to her room.

The diversion, shopping expedition and unorthodox re-entry to the hotel had cost her time and she realised he only had around ten minutes to disarm her computer and prevent it sending her violent request to eBay.

As Amelia arrived at her room, she searched for her room key, suddenly worrying that she may have left it in the discarded jacket. After a few moments of misgivings, she remembered he had transferred it to the backpack. She opened the door, crossed the room to the laptop computer, pressed cancel, then sleep. She gently unplugged the computer's connections and placed it, along with the mains adapter into the rucksack. Amelia briefly flicked through the other bag she had left in the room earlier, selected a few small items and then, carrying the old holdall in one hand and with the new rucksack on her back, she left the room.

Back at the Martinez, the Russian with the leather jacket had been watching from the rooftop. After ten minutes of looking, Amelia Brophy had not emerged. "There's something wrong," he said, "Amelia Brophy is still in the hotel." His colleague in the suit made his way, via the stairs to the ground floor. He looked around the lobby, restaurant and bar and then approached the reception. "Excuse me, my colleague was to call me, but I have forgotten his room." I am in room 729, with my other associate is in room 731. The person I am trying to contact is Ms Brophy."

The receptionist looked down. They would not typically give out room numbers, but the special guests in Rooms 729 and 731 had met a wide range of visitors over the last few days. "Room 610," the receptionist replied, "shall I connect you?"

"No that's fine, I will visit her instead". He walked back towards the elevators and called on his mobile. "Brophy is still in the hotel. She has a room."

There was a pause. "This is wrong. Finish it" said the voice. The neatly dressed man walked into the elevator, selected six and started the ascent. He walked to the room and then past it. He quietly pulled a sleek pistol from underneath his jacket. He quietly added the screw-in silencer and removed the safety catch.

Now he retrieved a golden coloured key from his wallet and inserted it into the lock. A small green light flashed; the door was opened. He slipped through the door into the dark room. He let the door close but had already flipped the deadlock, so that the door stayed ajar, but ostensibly closed.

He allowed a few seconds for his eyes to adjust to the low lighting, because the room was in darkness with the curtains drawn. He could see that Brophy was in the bed, an easy shot. Without waiting, he fired four rounds, three to the body and one to the head. The shots were almost silent, but the smoke and feathers created a cloud in the room. He quickly retreated, fearful that the smoke alarm would be activated and even worse the sprinklers.

A few steps later and he was back at the stairwell. The room's door was closed, a 'do not disturb' sign hanging outside. It should give until the next day before discovery.

He returned briefly to Room 731. "It's done," he said, "Do you want me to make the arrangements for Lambers, as well?".

Ten minutes later, he along with his colleague in the leather jacket, they were in a chauffeured S Class Mercedes on their way to Nice airport. They both held Belgian passports for this part of their work.

Sushi

Jake, Bigsy and Clare took the taxi to Waterloo and walked back to the venue for the rendezvous with the American. They had devised a relatively simple plan designed to keep some initiative with themselves during the meeting. They had arrived two hours early and were looking around the location of the restaurant.

The lunchtime rush was in full swing. They had taken up a position across the busy road from the restaurant. At 12:30, some thirty minutes before the arranged meeting time, Bigsy had crossed the road into the restaurant and taken up a corner position facing towards the door. As a sushi bar, it worked on a kind of 'as much as you can eat' principle, with little trays of food of varying types passing on a conveyor belt in front of the clientele. For Bigsy this was the ideal way to be involved in a stake-out, with continuing replenishment of food, "at elbow". He was most impressed.

The first part of the plan was simple. When the American approached the restaurant, Jake would recognise him. They had Clare's best camera with a long telephoto zoom lens and would also photograph him. Jake would do this while Clare walked into the restaurant to ensure that Bigsy knew what was happening.

During the period leading up to 13:00, several people entered and left the restaurant, some singularly and others in groups. Jake said to Clare that he found it challenging to be sure that the American was not in one of the groups.

Then suddenly at about one minute to one o'clock, he saw someone he recognised. Unmistakable. It was the American. tall, tanned, short hair, even wearing the slightly green looking suit. "That's him," exclaimed Jake.

Clare stood up and started to walk to the restaurant, not in a straight line from where they were sitting, but in a 'U' shape crossing the road at a pedestrian crossing. She strolled towards the restaurant, looking as if she was looking around for a friend.

Inside the restaurant, Clare looked around the table. She saw where the American was sitting and sat in the adjacent position. She looked as if checking whether her friend was in the restaurant. She blanked Bigsy, and he carried on eating some kind of rice and salmon dish, with chopsticks.

Clare selected a small passing portion of sushi and fiddled with a tiny clasp bag. The American watched out of the corner of his eye, while looking towards the door.

Clare pulled a paper from her bag and placed it on the table, as if about to take notes. Then she turned it over.

In bold print it said, "READ THIS". She gestured slightly towards the American who looked down momentarily and saw the paper.

It read as follows:

The Triangle

```
READ THIS.

FOLLOW THESE INSTRUCTIONS PRECISELY:

WE KNOW YOU ARE LOOKING FOR JAKE LAMBERS.

WE ASSUME YOU HAVE OTHER SUPPORT HERE. YOU MUST STAND IT
DOWN.

WE WILL LEAVE THIS PREMISES AND GO TO ANOTHER LOCATION.

DO WHAT IT TAKES TO STAND DOWN YOUR TEAM.

WE WILL THEN LEAVE TOGETHER.

IF WE ARE FOLLOWED, THEN YOU WILL NOT MAKE CONTACT WITH
JAKE.

WILL YOU CO OPERATE?
YES          NO
```

Clare pointed to the question. The American pointed to 'Yes.'

He stood up and coughed loudly three times. There was no sign of activity from anywhere else in the restaurant and the other diners, including Bigsy, kept eating.

As they made their way towards the door, they paid their bills, in fact, the American paid for everything, which Clare thought was something of a minor result. Bigsy noticed this too, and privately wondered how he could have got in on the act. He then snapped back into thinking about Clare's safety and started to prepare to leave the restaurant.

As he did this, the American said something to Clare, "He is NOT anything to do with me." Clare kept a straight face as they walked outside.

"Okay," said the American immediately they were outside. "My name is Chuck Manners, and I need to speak to Jake Lambers. He is in immense danger, and I think I can help. He also knows something which is of great significance."

Clare looked at the American, "Look we need your total co-operation," she said, "I am keeping you somewhere public. You are observed and being filmed right now. If you don't co-operate we will not allow you to contact Jake and we do need to know what you are doing. I am taking you to another location."

They walked, crossed a road and headed back towards Westminster. Jake took a steady stream of pictures from across the road but also noticed that there were no obvious signs of them being followed.

Bigsy left the restaurant about 100 yards behind Clare and the American and followed slowly. All three of them crossed towards Westminster Bridge and then made their way to the nearby County Hall complex, once the seat of Greater London's council and nowadays a Marriott Hotel. The long corridor walkway on the entrance was useful because it gave a view backward, which meant anyone following would be exposed.

Of course, this gave the American a chance to notice Bigsy. They walked into the hotel and found a seat in the bar. "Right," said Clare, "what is all of this about?" the American started again.

"As I said, I'm Chuck Manners, and I want to make contact with Jake Lambers, who I assume is your friend? I am here alone, although I believe that large guy over there eating the peanuts is following us. I also suspect he is linked to you in some way?"

Clare looked towards Bigsy and did her best to pretend not to recognise him. She thought that she was probably not convincing but kept up the facade in any case.

"My full title is Colonel Chuck Manners, and I am a fully serving member of the American military. I work for American Intelligence at present, although my prior time has been with the Marines. I am going to remove a document from my inside jacket pocket which confirms this. I will do this with my left hand and will move very slowly".

Clare was not ready for this development and a little stunned as he put his hand into his pocket and pulled out what looked like an American passport. Still using his left hand he opened it and inside the front cover was an individual declaration describing that Colonel Charles Jackson Manners was provided with diplomatic status and operated on behalf of the Government of the United States of America.

"I doubt if you will be convinced, even after this," continued the American, "I am involved in a major international investigation and the group of Arabs that Jake observed, along with the recently deceased Darren Collins are all integral parts. Jake is in great danger, and I think I have ways to be able to help him, but I do need to discuss this with him. I am not part of the recent killing of Darren Collins or Lucien Deschamps."

Clare was deciding the next action. "Okay," she uttered, "tell me what you think is happening."

"I will, but I need something in return," said Manners.

Clare asked, "and what is that?"

"I need you to get Jake to provide me with a copy of the digital transcript," replied Manners, "The version I have was damaged - but I know there is another copy."

"When we looked at the material on Jake's laptop, we saw that it had been backed up. Unfortunately, in the transfer from Jake's to our premises, the laptop had been left switched on and the disk drive had sustained some damage."

A waiter appeared, and they ordered two diet cokes.

Manners continued, "We were able to reconstruct most of the recording, but there are some significant gaps, including the section about the exchange of the code. We have created a replica of the section, which will keep our contacts busy for a few days, but we do need to give them a proper version."

Clare was looking carefully at Manners' face, for any sign of lying. She wasn't quite sure how she would know, but to her, it looked as if Manners was telling the truth.

"My role has been to infiltrate the group involved in the business of Darren Collins, the Arab team and others. It is critical to me that I remain undetected because we are on to a major international form of corruption."

Clare was also aware as these words came from Manners that she was sitting within short range of someone mixed up in some form of international crime and closely linked with extreme violence.

"We visited Jake's flat a second time to try to find the missing section, but when we looked around, we realised that Jake had created a backup system, but that the system had now been removed. It looked as if the removal was recent, particularly as there was a nice oblong break in the dust where the unit had been standing."

Clare listened as the story was unfolding. She was deciding whether to bring Bigsy into the picture.

"The point is," continued Manners, "that people involved in this via Darren Collins, or now via Jake, could all be in danger. The associates of the Arabs will stop at nothing to obtain that code.

"Until I met you today, I doubt whether anyone knows of your involvement. Now you and presumably that peanut eating friend of yours are also involved and become potential targets. Don't rely on the British Police to help you with this; they are as vulnerable as anyone else."

"But why?" asked Clare, "What is this about?"

"Look - I'll tell you some more, but if that guy is with you, then bring him over here, and I'll tell you both together."

Clare paused, and as she did so, she realised that the very act of thinking about it had told Manners what he wanted. He now knew Bigsy was part of it. She signalled to Bigsy. He approached, not sure what was happening. Clare briefly introduced them. Bigsy and Manners shook hands, and Bigsy sat down at the same table. The waiter appeared with two drinks for Manners and Clare.

"Here's the situation," said Manners, "The case we are involved with here is about international crime and money. There's a set of processes between organised crime and the way that the proceeds are made available."

"Laundering?" queried Bigsy, "we all know about that."

"This is more than laundering," replied Manners, "it's known as the triangle, and this is how it works..."

Manners continued to explain, "In normal society, there are many restrictions on money processing. For example, there is Sarbanes-Oxley, the Fed, the Bank of England, anti-laundering legislation in most countries and many cross border agreements and legislations. That keeps things under control but is not 'convenient' for two types of organisation. There are the very big legitimate organisations processing huge quantities of global transactions daily, and then there's organised crime."

"They both want roughly the same thing. A green lane. A lane, like on a toll road, that if you're pre-authorized, you can go through fast, without stopping, without excess paperwork, without having to get out the small change."

Manners sipped his coke, "So what happens? In an organised and commercial world, extra operational structures are created to help speed the transactions for global world trade. Big organisations get special authorisations, special dispensations and pre-clearances from government, national banks and other organisations to keep the wheels turning. For the right reasons this literally helps make the world go around. And of course, access to these processes is worth a lot of money. An absolutely huge amount of money."

Manners continued, "The other group with high interest in this are organised crime. At a global level, there are some organisations who want to do exactly the same thing as big business, but their motives are somewhat different. They start from a position where they have created a traffic in something which needs to be reprocessed. The simplest example is drugs, but there are many. The drug sales create money, we'll call it 'dirty' money. It can't be banked or used, but it accumulates at a tremendous rate. The second part of the process is to use 'green lane' style processes to convert the money from illegal businesses through institutions that look legitimate and onward into proper businesses. A part of the money stays 'dirty' and feeds back around the illegal system, and the rest flows on into surprisingly well-funded legitimate businesses."

Clare and Bigsy nodded. They had both seen movies about Las Vegas and using the Casinos to convert stolen money into clean money.

Manners smiled as he saw their look of recognition, "This isn't like the old Mafia days. The system nowadays is called 'the triangle' because of the way the money flows. At one point are the illegal organisations, at the second point the pseudo trustworthy organisations and at the third point the legitimate businesses."

"The people involved in this are huge consortia. We are talking about drug barons in South America, The '-istan' countries smuggling drugs and guns and anything else they can get their hands on, the Russian Mafia and some less scrupulous parts of the Gulf states, mixing oil skimming and other criminal acts together."

He looked at both Clare and Bigsy again; they certainly seemed to be taking in what he was describing.

"Yeah, this is huge," responded Bigsy. "How is it we don't hear more of this in the media?"

Manners continued, "The scale of this type of financial crime is huge, but it still only represents a small part of the total world economy. Increasing general knowledge of it only serves to further undermine other confidence in banks, governments and similar institutions."

"The NSA - that's the National Security Agency - in North America has been examining the parts of this which can be dismantled and the recent situation with Darren Collins was part of that. Collins had created an empire which was being used mainly by Arab interests who were taking money out of oil transactions and converting it into a mixture of legitimate and some illegal activities."

"Collins would never have been able to fund nor to establish his businesses without major help from people with a large bankroll but his recent situation was a consequence of his own greed and attempt to outwit the people controlling him. He already had a huge personal cash-flow and great margin on the business he was conducting but had tried to intervene in his own way to make more money for himself. It was stupid and was wrecking his empire and as a side effect drawing lots of undue attention to it."

Manners explained, "From an investigatory perspective, I was asked to get involved and to find out what was happening. It has been easier for me to align with the Arab interests and to treat the Collins situation as a way to get involved."

Clare summarised," So we've got a global ring of people laundering illegally gained money into normal money by passing it through fake institutions?" she queried, "and Collins was involved?"

"Yes, and already by now someone else will be setting up a new business empire to replace the one that has been destroyed by Collins," continued Manners.

"So how do you think Jake is involved?" questioned Bigsy.

Manners smiled, "Jake met Collins a few days before Collins was killed and just after Collins had been threatened by the Arabs. There's a high chance that Collins had passed something to Jake. Look, I know he did because I've got the recording from their conversation together. I don't believe Jake was involved before this. Also, the focus moves away from Jake as soon as the information is available. No-one is really interested in Jake; he is just a means to an end. Get him out of play. Provide the information."

Manners looked at them both. "I know you have the information. Or I know Jake has the information. Once I have possession everything can go back to normal. There's no point in further violence. We all just want to move along."

"Further violence..." was this a veiled threat from Manners?

Bigsy raised his eyebrows and looked carefully at Manners. "So why are you alone if this is so important? Where's your backup? Why haven't you just arrested us or something? You could take us to the police?"

Manners nodded, "You've worked it out already. I'm not exactly on the payroll of Uncle Sam nowadays. I'm acting freelance and working for the Arabs."

"They pay well and need someone like me who can 'get things done' with minimum fuss. You two, and Jake, are all in danger because of what they think you know about this.

"But I'm reviewing my options to get out of this. It's a treadmill, and I simply want a means to exit and disappear. Help me, and I help you."

"Give us a contact number for you," said Clare, "we will not give you the equivalent about us, though. We need to think about this and what we can best do. I can't say that we have the code you referred to, but if something comes to light, we will want to be able to find you," she added.

"I travel a lot," said Manners, "but here is a way to find me." He handed over a business card with his civilian name and a cellular number. The card looked like one that could be made in blocks of twenty in a stationery store.

"Trust me," commented Manners, "You are better to have a card like this, innocent and innocuous, rather than something which has 'Colonel Manners, Spy" written on it." Bigsy and Clare nodded.

"Time for you to leave," said Bigsy, "You go first; we will follow later." This made sense from a tactical standpoint. It gave Clare and Bigsy a chance to confer, but there was also a completely different exit available from the bar in the hotel, leading directly back onto the River Thames.

Manners paid the bill as he left the bar and as soon as Manners had walked to the end of the long walkway back to the street, Bigsy and Clare took the alternate route from the hotel and then melted into the many tourists walking along by the London Eye.

They walked further along the river past the street performers and crossed the river on the pedestrian bridge adjacent to the rail bridge leading to Charing Cross train station.

The bridge finished by the Embankment Tube train station which was also bustling with both tourists and working Londoners. They located a small Starbucks, situated or a corner and with a clear view of most of the area. Clare bought a tall skinny latte for herself and a grande cappuccino for Bigsy. They sat outside the cafe, in a cool early evening and waited for Jake to arrive through the exit from the station.

Chuck Manners had taken a cab to a small office behind Grosvenor Square, a part of London housing many embassies and with strong American connections. The office was behind an expensive but unprepossessing entrance in a block of similar residences. There was nothing obvious to announce the state-of-the-art technological interior. This was a monitoring station and had listening posts for several embassies, nearby cafes, clubs and coffee bars. If anyone in the intelligence or diplomacy world was indiscrete with information in the area around the prime embassies, there was a good chance that this would be monitored.

Manners wanted to be back to the tracking facility quickly. The meeting had taken nearly two hours, but he had achieved his objective, and interestingly he had also created an insurance policy.

He had considered it very unlikely that Jake would have appeared in person - he had been prepared for that, but anyway was less interested in Jake than in the whereabouts of the recording. During the first few minutes of meeting Clare, whilst still in the sushi bar, he had been able to place two miniature transmitters on Clare's clothing. They looked like tiny seed pods from a roadside weed each around the size of a grain of rice, rather than something high-tech and if Clare spotted them, she would be much more likely to brush them off, rather than to wonder what they were. And even better, the second one had been placed into the pocket of her jacket, a much harder place to find it.

And then when Bigsy had joined them at the table he had casually placed his jacket on the seat next to them making it easy for Manners to add a further two transmitters to the pockets of the jacket. He now had four available transmitters to give a signal and hopefully lead back to the site of the recording.

Jake was now approaching the Starbucks and spotted Bigsy and Clare sitting outside. He pulled up another metal chair to the shiny round table. Bigsy had just finished a slice of carrot cake and pulled the plate out of Jake's way. He carefully placed Clare's camera onto the table in front of them.

"I got some good photos," Jake said, "but when you all left for the hotel I had no idea what was happening. After Bigsy left, a couple of others left the restaurant within a few minutes, but they said goodbye outside and then walked away in different directions. The people after that caught a cab. I couldn't see any signs that you were followed. I really think Manners was on his own."

Bigsy and Clare concurred. They also had looked around for signs of others following them and also considered that Manners was alone. They explained to Jake what had occurred and about the idea that they were getting involved with something international and probably global.

"I don't know what to make of Manners though," said Clare, "He could be working for the Arabs, the US government or just for himself. It was impossible to tell. I would not want to have to guess whether he was telling the truth." Bigsy nodded agreement, although Jake thought Bigsy's face showed a different story. It looked as if Bigsy had believed every word of what Manners had said.

Jake's view was that they had stumbled into something big. That Darren Collin's death, Lucien's murder, the theft from his flat of his computer and the link of the Arabs and the American named Manners were all part of the same situation. The piece about 'the triangle' of illegal trade and money laundering was new information but was also highly consistent. So was the thought that he now possessed a key to another part of the puzzle.

Clare continued with her thoughts, "Manners just said that Police help and protection was not viable and that all three of us are now implicated. I think we have been pretty careful up to now and only Manners knows we three are all involved."

"Yeah, Manners and whose army!" added Bigsy, "If he really works for the Marines or the US Government, then we are probably all over their system by now".

"And if he works alone then we are probably not," added Clare. "If he works for law enforcement then I can't see why he would stop us from going to the police?"

"So, what next?" asked Jake.

"I have a suggestion," answered Clare, "How about this?"

Clare outlined a plan that they would visit the Zurich location from the internet web description, find out what was involved and then take it to the police as proof that something big was happening.

Jake would need to stay undercover. With only Manners knowing about Clare and Bigsy, they could move relatively freely, in the knowledge that if Manners had wanted to do something bad, he would already have done so.

They agreed their preparations over another coffee at the Starbucks and then headed back to Bigsy's flat, again by taxi. A short journey, they travelled together picking up a taxi from the cab rank outside Charing Cross station.

Manners watched their progress from the tracking room, his high clearance status with the Americans meant he could easily insert himself into one of the surveillance stations in central London. He had avoided the main embassy where the security was extra tight. A nearby facility was perfect.

The dots he was monitoring were travelling together and had paused in two locations. One was close to where the meeting had taken place, by Embankment Tube and the second was in a residential area. The dots were paused here for over two hours. Then they started to move again, this time, towards the Eurostar train station.

Being elsewhere

Amelia Brophy had decided to 'get the hell out of Dodge'. She was not sure how the Russians would react to her subterfuge at the Martinez, but she had a pretty good idea.

As she had met them but not shown them anything to trade, then there was a high probability that they would be on her tail. She decided to avoid the obvious route to London via Nice airport, but instead to work another route. She had to decide whether to simply finish the job with Jake Lambers, or whether she should first try to extract more information.

Amelia assessed that there was danger in either route, but that simply executing Jake would provide her with the Banker's draft she was expecting.

This would be a routine response from her current employer, and if she did this, took the money and then efficiently disappeared, it would be regarded by all as the end of her commitment.

On the other hand, if she started to dig into whatever secrets Jake held, then she was also sentencing himself to further pursuit and maybe elimination.

Amelia surveyed the local map to look for another suitable route back to the UK, other than via Nice airport. She did not want to use the roads back across France, which would take a long time, and there was a chance that she would be intercepted.

She decided to use Genoa instead, which was across the border into Italy. The drive from Cannes could be Autoroute for almost the whole journey, and she could do the drive in around an hour and a half. She would head for the Christopher Columbus airport in Genoa and then take a direct flight to the UK, or if there were any sign of delays, she would split the journey in either Frankfurt or Paris and then head back.

Her top priority was to get out of Cannes fast now, and she was keen to do this in a way that meant if he was followed that she had a chance to defend herself. Cannes is a prestige resort and getting a chauffeured car to Genoa would be easy and allowed her to break away from the Peugeot still parked by the Cannes train station. But she had also seen the selection of vehicles available to the rich and famous who stayed in the area.

There were small fast sports cars, expensive Mercedes and - her vehicle of choice - a Hummer.

The black Hummer was parked on the Croisette, with metallic detachable signage saying 'One Limo rental - A louer'.

This was an ideal vehicle for her journey. She could drive herself, had maximum protection should she need it and if she hired it for a week, there would be a long gap before the vehicle was detected as missing. Twenty minutes of paperwork, a false passport and driving license and a large credit card bill later, she had control of the vehicle. She had told the rental company of her plans to head along the coast. They had charged her extra for crossing the border into Italy, but were used to 'high rollers' who wanted to use flashy vehicles to smooth their way around the Cote D'Azur.

She fired the engine, confidently flipped the automatic transmission and moved off along the Croisette, turning right first into side roads and then nosing her way towards the Autoroute. She would be in Genoa within two hours, at the airport and seeking a flight towards London.

As she drove, she watched the sides and rear-view mirror; As she approached toll-booths, he looked around for cars idling to follow her. She was good at this. She was sure she was not being tailed.

The precautions of the huge black Hummer H2 were probably an over-reaction but, "Only the paranoid survive," she mused.

Bigsy's

Clare, Bigsy and Jake had returned to Bigsy's flat. They had decided that Clare and Bigsy would visit Zurich and check the apartment featured in the website. They suspected that a significant key to what was happening would be found if they did this. They were worried about Jake and decided that it was too dangerous for him to accompany them. Jake would continue to stay in Bigsy's apartment.

Clare left Jake and Bigsy for a short time while she ventured to her own flat to pick up some clothes and her passport. She collected a small backpack and a much smaller camera than the one she had used with Jake. She also dropped her own slim MacBook laptop into the rucksack and a selection of plugs and wires.

A short cab ride to Bigsy's and they made preparations for their hasty journey to Zurich. They were using the Eurostar train from London to Paris and then changing to a TGV Express train for the second section to Zurich. They considered the route to be fast to Paris and then after a change of stations in Paris; they would be on a fast train to Zurich. The route was direct but not particularly obvious, and they relied upon this to reduce the chance of being followed and certainly to reduce the possibility of being monitored, which would have been much easier if they had travelled by plane.

They checked their various phones, realizing that they only had two which would function internationally. Jake's could not be used; Jake continued to keep Clare's and Clare and Bigsy would share Bigsy's. The recently acquired "pay as you go" phone could only be used in UK and would also stay with Jake, but Bigsy insisted on taking Jake's phone, with the battery disconnected, in case they really needed a further international phone whilst they were in Europe. At least they could cross communicate, both by text and person to person.

"See you soon," said Clare to Jake. Bigsy winked, and Jake attempted to look amused back. All three of them were thinking that this could be a tough and uncertain few days. Bigsy and Clare, both carrying backpacks, then started their adventure on the way to the terminal for the next Eurostar express train to Paris.

Bad

From Cannes, the two Russians had soon reached Nice airport and, travelling on their Belgian passports, had caught the last flight back to London's Heathrow airport. They had arrived at around nine p.m. and decided to stay in a hotel close to the airport. They had the address of Jake's flat and would prepare to handle the situation with Jake in the morning. They used a shuttle bus to get to the Radisson Edwardian at Heathrow, which was close to the airport and also close to the main route running east from the airport into London, along the A4 trunk road and M4 motorway. From the hotel's concierge, they ordered a hire car to be available from the next morning, which they could use to get into central London.

By ten o'clock, they were in the hotel's brasserie, ordering a late meal and arranging to meet an associate for breakfast in a nearby venue.

Detective Inspector Trueman and Sergeant Green had decided to use the same morning to visit Jake's flat. They had already made several calls to his cellular phone as well as contacting his office. They had asked for an alert if Jake tried to call his office. They had also made a prior visit to his flat, and if they were unable to make contact on this occasion, then they would be taking a search warrant.

The Russians had started their own preparations to visit Jake's. They had started extremely early, picked up the hire car and driven from the hotel to an adjacent McDonald's burger restaurant.

Their plan was simple. If Jake didn't know anything about the plan on his life, then it would be easy to visit him while he was indoors and to finish the job. They knew that both Jake and also access to the information stored in his flat were important, with the trade-off that the information was paramount, and Jake was expendable.

In the neon-lit early-morning darkness adjacent to the McDonald's car park, they met their associate and transferred two aluminium cases from one car to the other. The exchange took a few seconds and both cars were back into the busy London traffic, the Russians heading towards London and the other car heading in the opposite direction, towards the West.

The Russians intended to execute their plan quickly. Visit Jake's flat; silently terminate Jake and then search the flat for the missing information. They knew that if Amelia Brophy had found the information, she would have used it to bargain during their meeting in France.

Without that, she had no leverage, she had failed a mission, not got paid and then faced her own execution. The two Russians would not make the same mistake. They had clear instructions with regard to Jake and also to the information that they required.

They would ask Jake for information first, rough him up second and if he was unwilling to divulge, then they would kill him anyway. If he told them the information, they would briefly verify it and then kill him. If he didn't appear to know anything, they would kill him and then tear the place apart. It was a simple plan, and the two end objectives were the termination of Jake and the retrieval of the missing information. They had planned the approach to Jake's to be early enough for him to be indoors and probably still in bed.

As they approached the area of Jake's flat, they surveyed the parking options. Central London, very early morning, residents still at home, so limited parking. They found a residents' spot and parked anyway. They realized the car may be clamped or worse towed away, but they knew that they could find an alternative escape route if needed.

From the back of the car, they opened the aluminium cases. Each contained a Pernach OT33 automatic pistol capable of firing eighteen rounds and the second case also included an army green holdall and a small bag of specialized tools. They took the tools, the two weapons and loaded them into the holdall. None of this was particularly heavy and the end result was easy enough to carry.

As they approached the house, they surveyed the parked cars in the vicinity. They were looking for something more than five years old. A red Vauxhall Carlton. This was easy. They quietly broke into the car, disabled the steering lock and ensured that they could start the engine. They now had two options for a getaway vehicle, as well as taxis and public transport.

They climbed the steps at the front of the house within which was Jake's flat, unaware that they were the third group to visit in this way. It was still early in the morning, and they made their way directly to his room. The Yale lock on the door was easy to disable. One of the tools in the smaller bag was designed to cut through the barrels in a household lock and to insert a new blank blade which could be used to turn the lock.

This made a small amount of noise, like a skipping power screwdriver, but within ten seconds the door was open. They both stepped in with their guns held alert, safety catches off. They could scare Jake witless before they started to question him. Like professionals, they moved swiftly from room to room, covering each other as they swiftly searched for Jake.

Nothing. No one present.

They both relaxed slightly and brought their guns down. Maybe they could find the information now and if necessary, wait for Jake to return later. The way they had disabled the lock was going to leave a tell-tale reminder that something had happened, so they realized at this stage that they were getting in deep.

One spoke, "Let's search for the recorder, or any computers which could store the information".

They started to search. It became quickly apparent that they were not the first people to work through the flat. There were enough mains leads and cables, spare keyboards and computer mice on the desktop to show that there had been one and possibly two computers there until a short time ago. There were dust marks from a fan inlet and some disconnected network cables, some of which ran to a junction box on the floor. Someone had been here and disconnected whatever technology had been present.

Trueman and Green were on their way to Jake's flat. This was their second visit. It was early morning, and if Jake was still living in his flat, he should still be there at the time they would arrive.

They had the same problem parking as the Russians. In their case, they parked in the same resident's area, but by flipping a small document onto the front dashboard, they had a different expectation from the Russians. They would not be towed away; their little card indicated they were from the local constabulary.

Together they climbed the steps to the main entrance to the house, which was already open. They knew the way to the flat, having visited previously. As they got to the door, they rang the bell but immediately noticed that the door was ajar and the lock looked damaged.

"Radio for some cover," whispered Trueman as Green pulled

his communicator from his suit. Trueman gently pushed the door open. He immediately saw the two men, who were both looking towards him. There was a staccato puff as the first bullet hit him, followed by two others. Before he fell, he saw Green walking backwards and then also falling to the ground. Two more bullets were fired and the room again became quiet.

The Russians looked at one another. "Whatever was here has been taken already - we should go." The second Russian nodded, picking up the walkie-talkie from Trueman's body.

"They were Police," he said, "We need to go right now".

They quickly gathered the tools and holdall and placed the pistols inside. The first Russian opened the door to the kitchen.

He turned on the four hobs and the oven and opened the oven door. Back in the area where the two police bodies lay, he lit a candle which was perched on a windowsill. He moved the candle further into the room and placed it on the floor.

"We have about five minutes," he said. They walked out of the room, closing the door. Then across the hallway and out of the front door, descending the three steps and back to their hire car, still parked in the residents' bay. The first Russian sat in the driver's seat, turned the ignition, and the two of them drove slowly away.

Seven minutes later, the police arrived, quietly, without use of sirens. The nature of the call from Green had suggested stealth and discretion. Two cars arrived, one ordinary police car and the other a more specialized armed response unit.

There were a few moments of radio exchange and then the men of the armed unit started to climb the stairs towards Jake's flat.

As they were preparing to go inside, there was a muffled sound like an explosion. It was the gas from the hob being ignited. The small blue-yellow fireball tore through the building. Immediate effects were the ignition of curtains and then cushions, the speed of the explosion was sucking the available air from the room. Blackened papers and other materials fluttered to the ground.

A steady blaze ensued as other items in the room also caught fire, more like a bonfire blaze now than the explosive nature of the first few seconds.

The armed police crouched and watched for respite from the fire, and then, as one, they noticed the prone bodies of Trueman and Green, just outside the entrance to what was rapidly becoming a blackened and smoke-filled room.

Ed Adams

Any place in the world

"It's a little monster."
Hummer advert, Super Bowl XL, 2006

Brophy visits London

Amelia Brophy had arrived in London the previous evening. The trip from Cannes, across the border into Italy, had been uneventful. The Hummer had been an exciting driving experience and Brophy, while keeping professional had been amused at this civilian version of what was an all-American military machine.

Amelia had used Hummers in the past (Hum-Vees in military slang), but this version was quite different with its plush seating and a 12 channel Bose stereo system. She knew it could still drive over another car if things got tough, or maybe push down a wall without losing its stride, but she had just used it as an expensive and very robust taxi to get to Genoa.

She driven it to the long stay car park, noted the bay number and would inform the company a day before the rental ran out. Her main objective in the short term was to escape general detection from the Russians as he made his way back to the

United Kingdom.

In the event, he was able to walk from the car park to the small airport at Christofero Columbus airport and select a direct flight with a lesser-known carrier back to London's Gatwick airport.

By evening, she had arrived, travelling light. She booked a room at the Gatwick Hilton, which was built right on the airport campus. From here, using the internet, she was able to accurately identify the location of Jake's flat and map out the surrounding area. Like the last victim at the gallery, this would be silent fast knife-work and she would be in position from early morning in two days' time to do this. Tomorrow was stake-out and the next day was execution.

In the morning, she had caught the Gatwick Express to Victoria and then caught a taxi to the general area of Jake's flat. Amelia had decided that if a direct opportunity appeared during the day, she would end it immediately, otherwise she would plan for a two or three a.m. entry to Jake's flat.

She rounded the corner into Jake's road. Immediately she noticed a police car, then a second, a police van, a fire engine and an ambulance. They were spread all over the road and there was a crackle from police radios.

Amelia looked along the road; certain this was related to her mission but convinced that no-one would know of her current plans. She started walking along the road, already creating her excuse to need to be at the shopping centre at the far end. A policeman walked slowly towards her.
"I'm sorry, Madam, I need to ask you to use another road this morning; this way is blocked. You don't know the people in the three houses over there on the left, do you?"

Amelia shook her head, "I'm just trying to get to the shops," he replied.

"You'd better go back to the corner and take the next road

then," the policeman replied, "we will be here a while".

"What happened?" she asked.

"You know I can't answer that," replied the policeman, "please just take another route this morning."

Amelia looked towards the central house, taped by the police. She noted the coroner, the fireman, the large number of police and that several had bullet proof jackets. She couldn't see any police weapons but knew there must be plenty in the close vicinity.

"Okay," she responded and started to turn. Then she noticed the red Vauxhall. Unlocked, wires exposed by the steering wheel. Wired as a precaution, a safety car.

"Not cool," she mused.

He turned back to the corner of the street and into another road leading towards the shopping centre. As she walked, she processed the information. A messy hit on Jake's flat, the very place he was targeting and less than two days after his discussions with the Russians. A botched and messy hit. A broken in and wired escape vehicle.

Professional attention to detail, but badly executed hit, drawing a lot of attention. This could only be the Russians. Unsophisticated but very pragmatic. She decided it was the Russians, probably the same ones she had met in Cannes, taking the short route to Jake. But why? It was her job.

This could only mean one thing. The thing Amelia expected had happened. They'd monitored for her to leave the hotel and when she didn't, they'd tried to locate her, found her room and tried to kill her. The way she had rigged the bed and the feathers had created enough confusion to mean the assassins had not checked but now believed her dead and the need to finish the job with Jake themselves.

She wondered if Jake had been killed. She had seen the coroner and the ambulance, but it was too risky to go back to check any further. Amelia was about to disappear and adopt a new name. This had got very personal with the Russians.

Eurostar

Clare and Bigsy were enjoying the train experience. There was something 'important' about travelling to Paris on the Eurostar. Many of the passengers looked like suited businesspeople on their way to meetings, flashing laptops, mobiles phones and all types of communication device.

Bigsy and Clare looked more like backpackers on the first stage of a long journey. They had been using their credit cards for ticketing and hotel bookings, and the ever-practical Clare had even told the credit card company she would be abroad to prevent the card from being stopped unexpectedly.

The miles and then kilometres sped by in a blur. Soon they were in Paris. Gare-du-Nord, and they now needed to cross Paris to the train station for Zurich. They used a taxi for speed and were soon in the new station.

A fleeting glimpse of the romantic city and they were again in the slight grime of a major train station, walking towards a sleek TGV which would take them to Zurich. In fact, the train looked more like an aeroplane and as they stepped into their second piece of luxury transportation, they both had to remind themselves that this was a mission, not a vacation.

Manners had been watching the cluster of dots on his surveillance system. The grain-sized transmitters were low power, and while ideally suited to monitoring movements around London, they limited traceability to within the Greater London area, bordered by the ellipse of London's peripheral M25 motorway. Bigsy and Clare slid out of London on the Eurostar. Other than the knowledge that they were on this train, Manners had no other way to track them across into Paris.

Manners could pinpoint a location when the transmitter dots had all paused at an address in Finsbury Park. With four transmitters, there was an accurate fix: Stapleton Hall Road, and an actual street number. From Google maps, it was a large house, converted into flats. Manners was getting organised to pay a visit. This time he would take a professional team, rather than the burglars he had used the first time to approach Jake's flat.

Manners was convinced that this address held the clue to the whereabouts of Jake and probably to the information he required. The travel of the two he had met in the Marriott was less impressive than getting to the coded data that was the basis for the reconstruction of the triangle network.

From his hotel near Park Lane, Fredriksson was also considering how to derive the code. He had the recording on memory stick from Manners and sure enough within this was an interview exchange which seemed to describe a code. Fredriksson knew that the code was supposed to lead first to 'the Blue Flame' but that the code number in the version supplied by Manners had an error. Fredriksson's attempts to second guess the missing code number was too difficult. All he had found was a long list of addresses, which looked like a range of churches in the North East of London.

Fredriksson paused to consider this; there was something wrong. Perhaps the recording had been manipulated? He switched to a sound analyser on his computer. He scrolled through the recording. The wave patterns showed some sudden changes as if they had been cut. This recording was a fake. Manners had doctored it. Fredriksson had no idea that this manipulation was done out of necessity, rather than as malice. Fredriksson made a mental note from this related to Manner's future.

He reached into his hand luggage and pulled out a pair of headphones. He plugged them in and re-listened to the last part of the recording. He could hear the almost imperceptible clicks as the sound had been cut and restarted. Fredriksson now decided to listen to the full recording on headphones to check for any other useful information or clues. For the first time, he listened to the first part, when Jake had been waiting for Darren Collins. Fredriksson used software like that which Bigsy had used, to boost the quality of the recording between Collins, the Arabs and Manners.

It gives you wings

Zurich, Switzerland. A pretty 10th-century town with a picturesque centre and beautiful views of the adjacent lake. Bigsy and Clare looked at the evidence of its origins. Of the wooden bridges decorated with flowers spanning parts of the central area with a history going back to the middle ages.

In the distance, they could see the outline of mountains, and they knew definitively that they were in a foreign country. For now, they needed accommodation and quickly found a Sofitel hotel close to the centre. They awkwardly discussed sharing a room but then decided to give one another space. Their credit cards were already quite dented, so decisions now would hardly make a profound difference.

In the event, the Sofitel was inexpensive, and they were both tired from the stress and travel of the day. After a brief meal in a nearby chain restaurant, they both collapsed for the night, ready to start fresh the following day in pursuit of the apartments listed on the website.

While Clare and Bigsy settled for the night, back in London Fredriksson was deep in the analysis of the original recording provided by Manners. He filtered and boosted the audio in the same way that Bigsy had achieved this a day or so earlier. Now

Manners could hear most of the conversation between the Arabs and Darren Collins, although it dawned upon him that sections were skipping which now sounded as if it was from a hardware fault. He also knew that Collins had continued the follow-up conversation with Jake Lambers, so if Jake Lambers could be found it provided the best chance to locate the missing information.

Fredriksson had no sophistication at his disposal to find Jake Lambers. Instead he looked for London phone directory enquiries on the internet and typed in "Lambers, J". There was just one. He could not believe his luck. He wrote down the address.

Manners was already planning his move on the located flat - he didn't know it was Bigsy's flat. Manners suspected that Jake and the needed information would be together at this address. He knew that the sleek woman and the large messy looking guy had moved away and that he would now have access to the flat and maybe Jake.

He was using a professional outfit for this entry. The two guys he had used at short notice for the previous break-in had damaged the stolen laptop even when stealing it from empty premises. This time he had personally selected a team. Americans, ex-military, used to working together, fast, professional and silent. Manners was in the right communities for this and could get people who would work for cash and not ask questions. Afterwards they would melt away and could be relied upon for their discretion.

The team he assembled for this was probably over-powered for the situation. He was using three men and himself as control. Four military onto one unarmed surprised civilian should be simple. They actually wanted the information, not Jake, so the objective had to be carefully proscribed to the team.

They planned an early morning entry to the flat, probably three in the morning when the occupants would be sleeping. They were going to use a surround pattern. Two through front access, one was covering back and a control across the road. This provided fast access, minimised escape routes and provided consolidation when they needed to search.

Two of the men would carry tasers. All three would have smoke canisters, and one would also carry a semi-automatic weapon. They would all wear daytime clothing with layers, so that if they needed to change identity it would be easy to discard a layer.

With their basic preparation, they collected the statutory white van which would form their primary transport. They also had another bland looking Ford hatchback which they pre-parked in the area. This was a 'B' car, to only be used in an emergency. It had been put in position the day before the operation. Two streets away were three pedal cycles, chained to railings as a third backup.

At one o'clock in the morning, the group of four were in the van. Manners and two of the men sat in the back. The fourth man drove. As they parked by Bigsy's flat, they pulled on balaclava hats. These were less to act as a disguise, but rather more to intimidate.

They synchronised watches, waited until seven minutes to two and then left the van to take up positions. Manners, acting as control, moved to the van's driving seat.

Inside Bigsy's flat, Jake was not asleep. Earlier in the evening, he had found a spare box of Red Bull caffeinated drinks, which Bigsy had stored on top of a cupboard. He vaguely recollected the poker evening about two weeks ago when they'd slightly overbought all of the drink and despite the attempts to finish everything, by the next morning they had all been sprawled around Bigsy's flat.

Jake had been trying to work out the possibilities of how the money laundering process operated. He supposed that the illicit activities could be from drugs, people trafficking, illegal gambling and other large-scale vices. The money could be flushed through casinos (simply lose it all and let the casino clean it up) but if there were significant enough quantities, even the casino route could become labour intensive. Having a process where the money was laundered through legitimate shell companies would make sense.

He found a large pack of flip chart paper and some big marker pens and started to draw the routing of the money. It did, indeed, look like a triangle of corruption.

It was around two a.m., but Jake didn't feel tired - in fact, the drinks had been giving him a real buzz to stay active. He decided to create a 'war room' about what had been happening, as he'd seen in the movies. It was this or to go stir-crazy. Wired with the excess caffeine, he decided that the sticky chewing-gum-like material known as 'Blu-tack' was needed to stick the papers onto the wall.

He flicked through Bigsy's kitchen drawers and the place where Bigsy's computers were stacked, but there was nothing suitable.

"Rick," thought Jake. "Rick the estate agent; estate agents are organised; he will have Blu-tack!"

Jake subconsciously recognised that this was a bizarre and somewhat illogical quest at two in the morning, he wondered if the drink was bringing out a latent obsessive-compulsive disorder. He wandered to the kitchen drawer and fiddled about at the back.

A key ring said "Foxtons"; it was Rick's spare keyring. Rick and Bigsy had swapped spare keyrings so that if either was locked out, they could borrow their spare sets to get back into their respective flats.

Jake remembered that Rick was away partying because the idea of paying a call at two o clock in the morning was beyond the normal description of neighbourly.

He opened Bigsy's door, leaving it ajar as he went into Rick's. The key worked first time.

He called "Rick?" just in case but there was no reply. He switched on the light and immediately switched it off again. He realised he had been working in semi-darkness for the last hour and that was about all his eyes could take. The light from the hallway was plenty enough. He looked around. He had visited Rick's before, a remarkably neat and well organised flat. In the general dimness, he walked to Rick's small office area and there, in a small box, was a selection of office supplies. Stapler, marker pens, erasers, computer CDs and, sure enough, a pack of Blu-tack. More than that, it was a pack of unused Blu-tack.

At that precise moment, he heard a huge bang. This was from the outside door and made him wonder what was happening.

The sound was the entry of the two intruders to the front of the house. He could see they were going directly towards Bigsy's room.

Jake kept a low profile. The noise he heard sounded as if it came from people who meant business. It could be that someone had now located him and was getting tough. He could see enough through the small gap in Jake's door.

The intruders had noticed Bigsy's open door and moved straight in. As they had walked into the entrance of Bigsy's, he could see they had noticed the spread of IT equipment on Bigsy's desktop. He noticed the third intruder making his way to Bigsy's room. They looked as if they were quickly checking throughout the flat, but there was no one present, just piles of paper and general mess.

The intruders would have their work cut out. Compared with

an average person's flat, Bigsy's had an exceptional amount of equipment. There were several PC towers, two laptops, spare disk drives and CD burners.

Jake decided his best option was to leave quietly whilst the Americans were in the flat. He slipped quietly from Rick's room, carrying Rick's spare Foxton key. Next to the flat key he noticed another one. It said 'mini' on it.

"Thank you," he thought, it was the key to Rick's estate agent's Mini, the one with the fancy paint job and the racing number on the side. As he left the flat, hecrept quietly down the steps, then he plinked the key on the fob, and a re-assuring double blip sound came from his left. It was the Mini, which now showed its taillights flashing and he sighed as he walked quickly towards it without looking back. He opened the driver's door, put the key into the ignition, turned it and then in a few seconds was manoeuvring the car out of the parked row of vehicles and past a double-parked white van.

Manners saw the car drive past, noted the registration number and waited calmly as the three Americans continued to search through the equipment in Bigsy's flat. A few minutes later, the first emerged. "There is a lot of equipment," he called, "Well, we have a lot of van," responded Manners. He knew that the equipment would be a faster way to the information and therefore more valuable than Jake. If he needed to do something further with Jake, this could be saved for another day.

Twenty minutes later, the equipment was on the van, and they moved away, driving through London to a small lock-up railway arch just south of the River Thames and near to Blackfriars. They would need to sift a lot of data now, to find the missing recording. Manners also knew the likelihood was that the recording would be easy to locate, simply by date added.

Ed Adams

To the dance?

"Dance as if you got lost
in the mystery and beauty of life."
— Debasish Mridha

Bouquet in Zurich

Bigsy and Clare had obtained a basic map of Zurich from the hotel concierge. They had found out where the apartment block was located and decided it was near enough to Central Zurich to take a taxi. The Zurich morning was crisply cold, but the sun shone. There was white frost in the shadows, but where the sun reached, it had melted and dried already. They had decided to keep the hotel rooms for two days so that they could use them as a base camp while they were on the trail of the Apartment.

Bigsy's phone rang.

"Clare" said the writing on the screen. It was Jake using Clare's borrowed phone.

"I'm in a jam," called Jake. "We've been rumbled at your place Bigsy," he continued and then began to explain the recent developments. "So where are you right now?" asked Bigsy, and Jake explained that he had borrowed Rick's car as an escape vehicle and driven out of London to the West.

He was parked in the Heston Services on the Westbound part of the M4 motorway.

"We'd better tell Rick about his car," continued Bigsy, "We don't want him blowing the whistle." Bigsy had the phone number of Rick on his cell phone and could call him after their conversation was over. He knew that Rick would be irritated rather than annoyed once he knew the car was not exactly stolen but rather that it was borrowed. He also knew that once Rick was in on part of the story, there would be total forgiveness.

Jake explained the situation to Clare, and they decided that it was best if Jake carried on along the motorway further out of London, and then found a cheap Travelodge for a couple of nights, until they got back and could rally their thoughts.

They agreed to keep in contact by cell phone and text message and then Bigsy rang off. Jake walked to the entrance of the Heston services building and saw a large road map of the UK, with Travelodges marked. There was actually one right here at Heston. This would do fine.

He walked back towards his car, and then drove the short distance within the services complex to the overnight Travelodge facility and requested a room for the next three nights.

Back in Zurich, Bigsy and Clare hailed a taxi, and made their early way to the apartment block that they had first seen on the internet site. Clare had a print of the details from the web-site and as they travelled she unwrapped it from her pocket.

"So how will we handle it when we get there?" she asked Bigsy. They had already talked about this. They would first simply visit the concierge if there was one and ask about the flat.

They would claim to have something to deliver. Clare thought flowers was the most straightforward. She could visit the desk and look like a florist doing a delivery.

Clare did speak some basic German, and in this area of Switzerland, a foreigner doing the delivery would not seem too out of place.

They had decided that even without a concierge, the flowers story would still be a good cover. They could then directly ring the bell to see if anyone was in. The apartments were big enough to mean there was reasonable traffic of people in and out, so getting into the lobby would be easy enough.

In the event, while they discussed these options in the back of their taxi, they soon found themselves at the apartments. There was the main entrance, with ground floor letterboxes and buttons to announce arrival.

This would make access to the building easy, but access to the specific Apartment quite difficult. They walked from the entrance back onto the main street. It was a fairly busy road with a nearby roundabout and a selection of shops, plus a bar and a separate cafe quite close.

Down a small hill was a further run of shops and close to the end of the row was a beautiful and decidedly high-end florist. Clare and Bigsy looked at one another and nodded. "This'll do fine," said Bigsy, "You choose the flowers, Clare!"

Clare selected a medium sized bouquet which seemed to be partly wrapped in some 'manly black' paper and without too many frills and bows. She then paid using some of the funny Swiss Francs, a mix of high tech bank notes and a type of coinage which nowadays seemed surprisingly large and heavy.

They walked back to the apartment block, entered the lobby, pressed the button to the Apartment and waited to see what would happen.

"Bonjour," said a voice.

"Hello," said Clare, "Sprechen Sie Englisch?" - do you speak English?

"Yes," came the reply, "I prefer to speak English rather than German," the voice continued.

"Great!" she continued, "I have a delivery of flowers for you." She was pleasantly surprised how easily this was going.

"Flowers?" enquired the voice. "Who are they from?"

"I don't know," answered Clare, realising they had not worked out this part of the plan, "It says they are from 'J'," she lied, thinking quickly.

"OK," said the voice. "You can bring them up". Clare looked at Bigsy, who had remained silent. This was going too well. Was this the right Apartment? Was there something else in play?

There was a buzz from an inner door, which now opened, leading to small elevator. Clare went inside, signalling to Bigsy to wait in the lobby. She ascended to the top floor and looked for the Apartment. There was another bell push on the door. She pushed it and waited for a response. Nothing. After a delay, she tried again. Still no response. At that moment, a different visitor appeared from around a corner at the end of the corridor and was making his way towards the elevator.

"Entschuldigen Sie mir," she asked, and continuing in German, "Do you know the person who lives here?"

"Nein," replied the man, who continued towards the elevator. She noticed he was wearing flip flop sandals and no socks. He also looked unshaven and unkempt. In her best German she continued and asked him if he knew any of the other people who lived on the floor. He briefly looked at her, looking up and down and at the flowers. "Es tut mir leid," he answered, "I'm sorry" and then continued in bad German to say, "I don't really understand German very well". As he said this, Clare realised that this was the same person she had spoken to on the apartment buzzer a few moments earlier.

"Look," she said, "I have come a long way to find you - I know about you and just want to talk." His posture softened, he looked as if he had received some sort of body blow. She realised it was an emotional response of relief, and she asked him if she could talk.

"Alright," he said, "You'd better come inside," now speaking English. Clare had a sense that she knew the voice from somewhere. They walked back towards the Apartment. "Wait," said Clare, "I must let my friend know what is happening". She pressed the fast dial on her phone and after around twenty seconds was connected to Bigsy, waiting downstairs.

"We are going to talk," she said, "I am also to ask him whether you can join us."

She asked the man, and he agreed to let Bigsy join them. He opened his Apartment door, pressed a buzzer and around a minute later, Bigsy stepped from the elevator.

"This is my friend Bigsy" introduced Clare, "and my name is Clare," she continued. "And my name is Darren Collins," came the reply.

In South London, Manners had already dropped off his three American assistants a short distance from their completed operation. They had then split up and made their separate travel arrangements. Each had been paid by Manners and knew that further questions would just increase risk.

Manners had now unloaded the computer equipment from the van. It was much quicker to unload with the van parked tailgate to the arch.

In around ten minutes, the equipment was spread in a row, while Manners decided how to proceed to interrogate it. He looked at what they had acquired. A few PC tower units, no doubt with large hard drives full of data; a couple of laptops, one quite old and the other very modern, some communication devices, a CD cutter and a small networked disk drive.

He looked at the disk drive again. It said 'Apple' on the top and someone had written 'Jake's Backup' in felt tip on the top cover. There was a good chance that this was the unit he needed. He started the modern laptop. It refused to co-operate. "Enter password," it blinked. This could take ages.

He looked again at the other equipment. He connected the various wires to assemble one of the tower units and switched it on. The screen was black and then some white writing flashed across. It was starting up. Around a minute later a blue screen winked 'welcome'. He pressed enter and it said, "Enter password". He tried the usual tricks, resets, special key combinations, passwords such as 'password, admin, secret, jake'. Nothing worked.

He decided he would need another approach. Picking up the small disk drive and its connector cables, he walked out of the lockup, and jumped back into the van. He was going shopping.

Please identify yourself

The news that Bigsy and Clare were talking to the previously assumed dead Darren Collins was a complete shock. The three of them hurried into the apartment, which was sleek and stylish. Clare remembered Jake's words about Darren's office. How elegant and cutting-edge it had been.

This description also fitted the apartment here in Zurich although the current version of Darren standing in front of them didn't. They had never seen Darren before, and so they only had his word that he was who he said he was.

Clare realised that he and Bigsy were accidental experts on a small slice of Darren's life. His car. They had both listened to Jake's interview two or three times, looking for clues. If this was Darren, he should be able to give the same answers about his pride and joy motor vehicle.

"So, before we start," quizzed Clare, "we need to ask you some basic questions. They may seem strange at first."

"Go ahead," said Darren, "I could predict this".

Clare started to ask questions about the McLaren car. Starting with simple ones about what type of car was it, and then progressively getting more specialised, based on what she could remember from the interview. Maximum speed, number of cylinders, the way the doors opened, and Darren was getting them all right.

Bigsy realised what Clare was doing and also nodded as he heard a series of right answers. Then Darren asked a question, "So what colour was the car?" he asked the two of them. Neither knew. It was not in the interview. They hesitated. Darren said, "I thought so - you are working from the interview transcript - Is that where you got this apartment? - and what has happened to Jake...er...Lambers?" he quizzed.

"Jake is fine," answered Bigsy, "and we needed to know you were who you said you were before we went any further. How on earth did you get here, and what is the story about you being dead? - This is all very weird..."

"Weird, dangerous and complicated," responded Darren. "I will explain, but I need to know I can trust you first" - he walked to a wardrobe in the room and returned with a small metal box. Inside the box was a passport, a badge and a cell phone.

"I was recruited to a special unit within HMRC - Her Majesty's Revenue and Customs. Because of my tax status, they made me an offer I couldn't refuse. HMRC has a special operations unit, involved with international crime and international fraud. I was working on a highly sophisticated crime involving drugs, vice, major currency movements and money laundering."

"We had worked out it was something illegal," replied Clare, "We have been putting together our theories," she continued.

"Let me try to explain," responded Collins, "There's a lot to tell - I'm trusting you two; if you'd wanted to harm me, you'd have already done it by now. The story stacks up that you are friends of Jake Lambers. But understand me; the more I tell you, the more dangerous it gets for all of us."

Collins moved across the room to a bright area with two colourful yellow leather sofas facing one another and separated by a table made from some kind of grey stone. The table looked immensely heavy and probably cost as much as Bigsy's car. On the wall between the sofas hung a huge sleek plasma television.

"I was part of an undercover investigation. UK Government asked me to embed myself in the unit under investigation. The powers of the Customs and Excise in the UK are some of the most powerful in the British justice system, so I could operate in ways which were well outside the powers of the police force, for example. That's not to say I was going out of my way to break the law, let's just say that it became a necessary extension to find out the scale of what was happening. I had to get sign off from the Home Office, although even that creates problems for me now."

Clare and Bigsy looked at one another. Either they were being told the truth, or this was a wildly elaborate lie, for reasons they couldn't fathom.

Darren continued, "I've been tracking a massive money-laundering operation. I had to set up a new 'node' in their network and become part of the process. Their name for the network - alshuelat alzirqa' - the blue flame.

Bigsy interrupted, "As in the Blue Flame code word?"

"Exactly," continued Darren, "Using the Blue Flame as a code was a way to tell people involved with following up what I'd been doing that they were on the right track.

"Except no-one could say the Arabic. We decided to simplify, and it became Almathlath, which most people could spell well enough in reports. It means "The triangle," in Arabic.

"Everyone I was working with knew about Almathlath as a code word, so when I used the Blue Flame and a code number, it gave a way to confirm that it was linked."

"Isn't it all a bit 'over the top'?" asked Clare.

"Trust me," continued Darren, not realising the irony, "We are dealing with some heavy people here, and they don't mess about. If they take a dislike, then someone is going to get killed."

"Yes, we've seen that already," continued Clare.

"So, Blue Flame is an organisation making money on an industrial scale from the illegal export of petrochemicals from Saudi Arabia," explained Darren. "There are several aspects, and the processes for each of them are pretty much the same. I'll explain it with oil, but it applies to other commodities too."

"It can be deceptively simple. Oil products are drilled, pumped and processed in the normal way in the eastern part of Saudi Arabia, but the supplies are then split in their transit towards the port for onward transmission."

"The legitimate part went through the normal port side and customs clearance, but the illegal part was simply split off and continued in different pipelines until they reached another sea-based destination. There are underground pipelines from two large Saudi ports at Al Jubayl and Ras al Khafji. One simply goes to an obvious offshore fuelling point but the other snakes across the border into neighbouring Iran."

Bigsy and Clare's geography was not up to the level of the description from Collins, and they stopped him to ask some questions.

"Just a minute," answered Collins and he flipped a remote control laying on the stone table. The plasma screen flickered into life. "It's an internet terminal as well as a television," commented Collins, "let me show you." He flipped a couple more buttons and reached down by the side of the table.

There was a sliding drawer, and he pulled out of it a slim white keyboard and a small white mouse. He placed both items on the table and started to type. The screen now showed a conventional-looking computer display and then up popped an internet browser display. He tapped "CIA Worldbook" into the keyboard, and sure enough, up popped a screen saying "CIA World Fact Book".

"This is a CIA website," he explained, "but anyone can use it. For field operatives, it is easy to flaunt some of the access to systems rather than hide them. If an agent in the field needs access and doesn't have specialised equipment, then the Criminal Intelligence Agency has made it easy to get basic information."

He continued and tapped in "Saudi Arabia", and within a few seconds, he was on a screen showing basics facts and figures about Saudi Arabia. A few more taps and he was looking at a map of the region.

"Look, here," he continued and gestured to the western side of Saudi Arabia on the map and then to an area around the Persian Gulf.

Here, they could see the towns Darren had referenced. Bigsy and Clare could see that they were well-positioned for access to the sea and near enough to the borders of surrounding countries.

"The investigation I was involved with started by looking at these very spots," he gestured to Al Jubayl and Ras al Khafji.

"The basics were that fuel oils were coming into the UK illegally, often from Southampton and Liverpool. There was a trail that led back to the Gulf, and the good customs people were investigating the basis of the route. At the time it started, they had no idea of the scale or reach of what we had discovered."

"Our unit asked me to get involved as a way to gain intelligence about the scale of the operation. My trading operation at the time was iffy, and so I was given a front as a trader susceptible to corruption. Someone then introduced me to the Blue Flame crowd, and I was later approached to extend their operation."

"By whom?" asked Clare, "Surely you are provoking the illegal traffic rather than stopping it? Isn't that 'entrapment' or something?"

"You have a point, but at this stage, I didn't have a clue about the eventual process I would discover and though it would be more like a simple sting - you know, they hand me some money, I call in backup, and everyone gets arrested!" continued Darren.

"Except it wasn't like that. They approached me via an intermediary representing offshore interests and created a complete legal framework from a company based in Belgium. I was asked to participate by a Swedish businessman who was fronting a consortium of Arabs from Saudi and the other Gulf States."

" I think the people I met believed I was already involved with some other financial crimes. We used that to provide me with a stronger background story, and corroboration, both in police files and with other places we expected would get an investigation."

"The Swedish businessman was named Fredriksson. He made me the offer that became the basis of the operation that I was running when Jake met and interviewed me. I had to opt-in as a way to follow the trail and frankly was not sure about what would happen to me if I declined."

Bigsy and Clare both considered the implications of what they were hearing and tried to work out whether it was all true. A lot of it tied up with what they had heard from Jake, and with theories they had been working out between themselves.

"So how did you get the money to create the office and

business that you were running?" asked Bigsy.

Darren replied, "It was amazingly easy once they had decided they wanted me to do this. I don't think I can easily describe how much money is involved in this process. Imagine an oil field which is permanently pumping its product into an illegal operation. The operation of the oil field is part of a legitimate operation which passes all the normal tests and inspections. The only difference is that the declared capacity of the oil field is only half of its true output. The rest disappears into the illegal process. Now multiply that by many fields. You should be starting to get an idea of the volume of money in this process."

"Using me and asking me to create a shell organisation to start the laundering process just created more and more cash. To begin with, I couldn't believe how much money was created, although my main interest was to follow the chain back so that we could round up the people responsible. I had to make the operation I was running look suitably big and stylish to convince them of my character as we had to create the right sort of attention."

Clare and Bigsy looked confused by the last remark.

"We needed to attract a particular type of attention so that if there were other equivalent organisations, there would be a reasonable chance to flush them out. The car article was more than just self-promotion - it was also planned as a commercial about what we were doing, to people in the know.

"Journalists like Jake may not realise it, but some of those glossy magazines are also recruitment and advertising spaces for organised crime. Spot the bling. We all know what a Rolex means, but there are other subtle signs as well. Vacheron Constantin could indicate Mafia connections. Pobeda watch, a Russian patriot - possibly connections to FSB. Do you get my drift?

"We'd realised that this particular organisation was like the tip of an iceberg. We found out that there were other organisations also operating in an interconnected way, using similar processes to launder their own money. Organised crime needs a way to re-introduce its money to the economy, and this approach seems to be a widespread thing." He paused.

"So, from starting to track down some oil tanker mischief in Liverpool for HMRC, I became more involved with it as I got deeper into their crime syndicate. I was beginning to see the scope and breadth, but I also realised that I was also becoming more and more of a target if I attempted to report back my involvement. The session with the Arab heavies that Jake Lambers spotted was a turning point for me."

"That's when I decided that I needed to get out or be in fear of my life. My way out needed to be via a plausible exit of some kind, but in a way that escaped complete detection. I had to do two different things. One was to create my separate fund so that I would be able to create a new and utterly independent life for myself. With the access to money that I had, a small adjustment to a couple of the dials would very rapidly create a fund for me to use in a way that was pretty much undetectable. The second thing I needed was to create a plausible reason for people to stop looking for me - hence the car crash story".

"But the way you describe this it makes it sound as if you've turned from 'one of the good guys' into 'one of the bad guys'," questioned Clare.

"It has become a matter of survival for me," replied Darren, "If I blew the whistle on what was happening, I doubted whether I'd make it to the next weekend," he said.

"The people involved with this have an exceptional reach, and with such funding, any minor hindrances are ruthlessly dealt with."

Collins went on to describe the complicated way he had engineered his disappearance. He had manipulated some failures the business and simultaneously been moving money away in preparation for his demise. Collins had also used his background to get himself interviewed. He wanted someone random to meet him and to use this to pass on some details. He was going to use this random factor to create a way to complete the chain of feedback without traceability back to himself.

"So, we are the chain?" stuttered Clare

"Correct," replied Collins, "there was supposed to be no link between Jake and me. Now you've come along it adds even a further stage as you are not the person who interviewed me about my car. And when you pass the information on to the people I tell you, you will need to think yourselves about how to add another link".

Collins continued, "There is a considerable amount of data to describe the network of links; it is similar to the internet, in that if one part breaks, another route is used as a diversion until the original link heals in some way.

"The size of the network means there are ways to cross-check things. That is one of the reasons it had to look like a road accident."

"Well, you certainly fooled most people," said Bigsy.

"Yes, and we didn't even know it was you when we figured out the co-ordinates from our code-word," said Clare.

"I had to use a substantial sum of money to create what is essentially an alibi based on my faked death.

"Anyone from the dark side of this network would take no chances after such a fabrication."

"Meaning what, exactly?" asked Clare.

"They would also kill the people involved in the cover-up so that there was at least one further layer of insulation to get to the truth. I didn't do that, so there is always a chance that I will be discovered as still alive by someone from inside Blue Flame."

"Now I'll have to make the best of things. I'll pass you some information which together will allow the network to be detected and attempts made to start to dismantle it.

"The reason I can do this is that I was operating on such a large scale that I started to find out about more than one operation of the system. By the time I had access to three routes, I could start to piece together how the whole environment has been created."

"You mean like triangulation?" asked Bigsy.

"In a manner of speaking," responded Collins, "if you start to assemble the network, particularly in the European and North West Asian area, then it is possible to start to see where the trunk routes of the money flow. I said it's about more than oil and it does seem to be much broader."

"Everyone expects that the Russian mafia is also involved and that there is influence from the drug traffic from Pakistan and Afghanistan's Helmand Province which flows across to Turkish connections."

"The Arabian part links with the illicit oil shipments and that is the area where I was first involved. Of course, this only represents one-eighth of the planet and doesn't even touch the United States, or South America, so I expect there are other large zones which are not even visible at present."

"The data I collected from the inside is stored on a hard drive. If I deliver it in its current form, I am certain that many people I know will be killed as retribution. We need to find a way to achieve the delivery of the data without making it so obvious about the source."

Clare asked, "So you will give the information to us? - won't it have the same effect when we try to pass it on? We may deliver it, but it will look the same and therefore link back to you?

"Precisely," said Collins, "That is why you must change the information first".

"The most straightforward way will be to use the information I have provided to pass to another new organisation. It can be done in a way that ensures interception by a government agency and becomes the plausible way for Blue Flame to be discovered.

"The trick is to do this very early in the start-up of a new organisation. The recipient won't understand the information they are getting, but the authorities will. We can add a few keywords to prove authenticity, without it being obvious that I've been involved, or that any of you are either."

"That way, the authorities get what they need, but none of us is implicated".

Clare and Bigsy remained silent as Collins stopped his description; in their wildest imagination, they could not have foreseen the events or stories of the last couple of hours, even on top of the events of the previous couple of days.

"So you are telling us that you are sitting on the key to breaking the organisation, but can't use it directly?" asked Clare, "If you do, they'll work out the source and then everyone linked will be in trouble."

"Correct," said Collins, "But using my plan means that the source is completely concealed, via the new organisation acting as the unsuspecting deliverer of the information. And it moves the trail away from all of us, completely."

A hands-off approach

Fredriksson had slept until late the next morning. Although only a few hours hop from Riyadh to London and with the time zone working in his favour, it was still disorienting. He had left Riyadh on a plane at around 0200. Then, arriving in London's early morning after not much sleep, on top of his already hectic schedule meant that he decided to take some downtime.

He had located the address for Jake's flat, but obtaining Jake's information was of secondary importance to him. He would be starting the process to build a new node relevant to the business, to replace the area taken down by Collins. He knew that Collins would have a safety net of some description and he considered that he also had factored similar things into his own plans.

Right now he had the commission to activate some of his own existing trading entities to provide the new transfer medium for the money in line with the need of the Arab consortia.

Fredriksson did most of his work through others and had many operating guises through the companies he ran. There was a degree of legitimate business included, and the diversity meant that he had easy access to a wide range of employees, from top-quality legal and financial advisors through to manual labourers.

Fredriksson was used to getting what he wanted and could use a discreet viewing of Jake's flat and maybe Jake himself, to determine the options available. This could veer from gentle persuasion, through a job offer to violence or even worse, depending on the circumstances that Fredriksson detected.

Fredriksson also considered the visit to determine Jake's whereabouts as something of a scoping exercise. He thought that probably Jake was harmless and maybe an innocent bystander. Within a couple of days, the remnants of Darren Collin's empire would no longer be relevant. Although there would be vestigial companies and paper trails, most of what was important would have disappeared. His people were good at that and would speedily create a substitute 'node' to continue the job where Darren Collins had left off.

Fredriksson was one of the people least concerned about any aftermath from Collins. The effects of Collin's companies did not touch him directly, and there were no links back to him, although he had previously taken a direct hand in their creation.

Fredriksson would financially back the start-up costs of the replacement but would take a similarly 'hands-off' approach. In all ways, that is, except he would get new creation fees for setting up the replacement routes, and that he would continue to get a modest small proportion of all of the money that transacted every day.

And that was millions for him just through the part of the network which had been operated by Collins.

Fredriksson enjoyed a brief breakfast in his hotel room; yoghurt, brown bread and a small slice of cheese, washed down with two cups of strong coffee. He was in the business part of the hotel, with a medium-sized room with some in-room office facilities. Fredriksson's black suit bag and minimal luggage hung directly in the open plan wardrobe. He could be in this location for two or three days. It had some anonymity, was not overly flashy and helped him to blend in when he needed to.

His next route was to take a taxi to the area of Jake's flat. He left the hotel and picked a cab waiting outside. The black cab took him to the area of Jake's flat, but he had asked to be dropped a couple of roads away. Like Amelia Brophy before him, he then discovered the still unfolding aftermath of the Police visit to the flat.

He was several hours later than Manners and decided not to make direct contact. It was obvious something unpleasant and violent had happened, and whether or not Jake was still alive and whoever else had been involved, Fredriksson simply registered that there was ongoing interest in Jake and that he, Fredriksson, needed to move quickly to take down the old network and to establish the new one.

He flipped open a slim black cell-phone, pressed a power-dial number and waited. A few seconds later, there was a click, and the number was answered.

"It's Fredriksson," he declared, "I have the go-ahead, and we will need to move fast. We need to meet somewhere neutral, in central London."

A few minutes later, they had agreed to meet in the Foreign and Commonwealth club, located centrally, a few minutes' walk from Trafalgar Square, in Central London.

Manners on a mission

Manners was used to working in counter espionage. He knew the moves. He could tell now that he was working with a combination of technique, but right now it was mainly 'luck' that was winning.

The disk drive he had picked up from the collection of electronics at the flat was different from the other equipment. Most of the stuff was PC related. This single item had an apple logo and also had a label saying 'Jake' on it. Manners was confident that this would contain a backup of the broken Apple MacBook which had been delivered to him by the clumsy burglars.

He had tried to read it with all of the available PCs at his disposal but would now need to get an Apple computer to try the drive. He was on his way to a nearby PC superstore. He would buy an Apple laptop and then connect the drive. He was sure this would work.

Two hours later, he was sitting in a small hotel room close to Oxford Street, with the new cardboard packaging from a small slim silver laptop computer scattered on the floor. The machine was switched on and powered up. It displayed a blue background with four simple icons and a narrow strip with further images running along the bottom of the screen.

He connected power to the disk drive from Bigsy's, he pulled a cable from some bubble packaging and plugged one end into the disk drive and the other end into a socket on the side of the slim computer. There was a moment's pause, and then a new icon joined those already displayed. It was a small picture of the disk drive,

The laptop had found the disk drive and connected to it. He clicked on it and found Jake's backup file structure, from Jake's laptop computer. Manners clicked a couple more times and found the folder containing the list of digital recordings. He located the correct file for the data he wanted and then clicked again.

The sound of the recording stated to come from Manner's laptop. It was the recording, this time it was undamaged and pristine. He listened to all of it and made a few notes along the way.

"Computers for the rest of us," he mused thinking of the simplicity with which he had fired up the Apple laptop to achieve this.

The most important note he wrote down was the reference to the secret code. This was the one that he had been unable to hear in the earlier recording because of the damage. This time the code was clear. He listened, wrote it down, rewound that section, listened again and cross-checked with the earlier recording.

Manners knew he had the right code. He then dragged the picture of the folder containing the digital recordings to the desktop of the laptop computer. He now had the files on his laptop, where he could inspect them at leisure.

Manners was now ready to hunt down the source of the number. He was on the trail of whatever Darren Collins was hiding.

Fabric

Jake was beginning to go a little crazy. He had been locked up in Bigsy's flat for two days and had then nearly been caught by some people who were looking for either him or the equipment and files he had been holding.

He had managed a lucky escape using Rick's car and was now in hiding somewhat anonymously in the Travelodge along the M4. He had called Rick to explain what had happened, using Clare's phone and as he had started to explain, he decided to let Rick in on more of the recent events.

Rick was not very phased by what he heard. An estate agent by day, Rick spent the evenings enjoying the single life in London and was often out clubbing. He met many people in his varied exploits and there were always Londoners with stories to tell.

On the club scene, or particularly on his club scene, there were always people showing that they were connected to big things in some way or other, so Jake's story sounded like other ones he had heard. Except, as Rick put it, there was a first-hand experience of people getting killed in Jake's story. And Rick also knew Lucien a little bit, so this had an extra edge compared with the stories of his clubber friends.

Jake asked Rick if they could meet somewhere so that they

could discuss this in more detail. It needed to be somewhere secure and preferably somewhere that Jake could visit without too much chance of getting followed.

"We'll meet tonight," said Rick, "Fabric, in Farringdon. No one will get in there without an invitation. Take my car to Heathrow Airport, park it in T5 car parking and then come in by train tonight."

Jake was pleased to receive this direction and plan from Rick. He had felt somewhat out of the action over the last couple of days, stuck at a motorway service while Bigsy and Clare were in Zurich. His action had been limited because he was the one under threat. Not being able to do much, not being able to communicate quickly and being the potential target of a threat did not leave him feeling particularly safe.

He was aware of the possibility of paranoia, but decided nonetheless, to visit a local shopping centre on the way to the airport parking zone. He visited a department store, bought a complete change of clothing and then, after paying, slipped into a nearby McDonald's where he changed from his existing clothes into an all new set.

His new clothes (black jeans, black tee shirt, and dark hooded jacket) were deliberately commonplace and anonymous and included a new backpack with a couple of further items so that he could change his appearance quickly if the need arose.

As he did this, he was thinking that he might be going mad, but on the other hand, it was better to be safe than sorry.

Next stop, Terminal 5 Heathrow, where he could park for a huge daily amount, and he left the car in the middle row of a busy section.

The vehicle was distinctive, but you couldn't easily see it where he had parked it unless you were already inside the parking lot. He realised that there would be number plate recognition at the airport so the car had limited time before it would be discovered if it was on a watch list. He wrote down the zone but left the ticket in the glovebox and walked through the vast car park and across the concourses into Terminal Five.

Then a Heathrow Express to Paddington and Circle Line to Farringdon, where he would meet Rick. As Jake stood on the tube, he looked at the mass of Londoners and thought how good it was to be anonymous.

PART THREE

Killer instincts

Jimmy was the kind of guy that
rooted for bad guys in the movies

— Henry Hill (Ray Liotta), GoodFellas

Amelia gets personal

Amelia Brophy was still in London. She had decided that the chaos around Jake's flat was Russian inspired. Amelia knew the modus-operandi of the Russians and their more basic level of training. She was normally very dispassionate about her work, but she knew for sure that the only reason the Russians would be handling the situation with Jake Lambers was because they thought they had killed him back in France.

Amelia had been careful with his hotel room preparations back in Cannes. She had set a trap, based upon what he knew would be a lot of smoke and feathers following any attempt to 'assassinate' whatever lay under the bedclothes in the room. She had set up the bed carefully, so that anything fired into the simulated mass of his sleeping body, would cause the assailant to leave hurriedly.

She therefore knew that the Russians would have thought they had killed her and were now attempting to finish off Jake.

Amelia decided she would now create some disruption on the

way to capturing the ringleaders of the attempt on her life. She considered it very uncivil to one minute be offered drinks and the next for the same people to be regarding her as target practice.

Amelia needed to set a trap if she was to capture the Russians.

She started by phoning a number in Saudi Arabia. Someone he knew who would be looking for large amounts of extra cash.

She was going to create a scene in London designed to jeopardize the very operation at the heart of her contract.

They were playing rough with her; she would do the same back to them.

She was going to create a situation where two parties both thought the other had the data that Jake had acquired.

Amelia didn't need the information any longer; she was going to create some havoc to send a signal that she didn't want to be messed with.

Amelia knew her actions would be seriously irritating two major international players, and she needed to be careful how he handled the situation.

Her move would be to pretend to each group that she was working for the other side.

By calling the Saudi Arabian contact, she was telling them that she had information about the whereabouts of the coded data which Darren Collins had produced, and which Jake had subsequently recorded.

She then did a similar call, but this time to the Russians. She explained that she had the disk and the data which they needed.

Aware of the fireworks it could create, she invited both groups to meet her in London.

Dillon, sounds a bit like Collins?

Fredriksson made his way to the Foreign and Commonwealth Club near to the Embankment in central London. He would be meeting a new associate there, one who came highly recommended and for whom Fredriksson had already run comprehensive checks to validate.

He knew there were a couple of suspended meeting rooms in the Club, on the first floor accessed via a walkway. They added a sense of drama to the meeting he was about to conduct. He had selected one of these rooms for the meeting and deliberately arrived early to take a seated position facing towards the door of the meeting room.

At the appointed time, his guest arrived.

Fredriksson knew that his guest would be accompanied, but that courtesy and protocol would mean that whoever else he had brought would be waiting downstairs.

"Mr Dillon," he said as he greeted his guest, "so good of you to come."

Dillon was a well-known man-about-town. His profile was a little flashy, and he featured frequently in the tabloids and weekly magazines.

He had made money from music and fashion and had a whole string of companies and miscellaneous interests.

Fredriksson had met Dillon before on two occasions and had been weighing up the possibilities of using him as a new part of the laundering operation.

Fredriksson had decided to split the previous 'node' operated by Darren Collins into two pieces. He was using upscale interests for one part and needed someone else who could front the more ragged elements of the Collins empire. That is where Dillon came in.

Fredriksson spent the next forty-five minutes speaking to Dillon. He explained that there was a large sum of money to be made, that the income was regular and that the nature of the business transactions was mainly virtual.

Dillon did not need to hold stock, and Fredriksson's associates would supply the necessary processes for the transacting of business.

There would be a need for some specific undertakings from Dillon, including a clause that permitted rapid revocation of the whole deal in the case of anything untoward. This had to be pre-signed and was an unconditional aspect of the negotiation.

Dillon listened intently to the offer. He was very interested and had been hoping that something like this was possible, based upon the previous discussions with Fredriksson.

He knew that there were probably shady aspects to the deal, but many of his other agreements were also border-line, so this was no significant exception.

He explained that he would need to consider and to check with his legal people and that he needed a small amount of time for this. Fundamentally Dillon believed that he was asked to be a clearinghouse for someone else's money and that he could take a percentage of the money.

The offer was highly attractive to Dillon, but he realised that there would also be some downside and that that this probably relates to personal risk.

"Do this well, keep a low profile in these transactions, and you will have nothing to worry about," came Fredriksson's reply.

Dillon and Fredriksson agreed to meet again two days later to finalise the arrangements. Fredriksson was close to restarting the entire Darren Collins organisation under its new management.

Sand and vodka storm

Amelia Brophy had decided to create a big storm in London. Always professional, she had taken the recent attempt to kill her as both a personal situation, but also a professional one which required deflection.

Creating an incident where two sets of oppositional people were "accidentally" introduced to one another would create a distraction, and she could also usefully study the aftermath.

She had already called both groups. The point was to get them to the same location in the knowledge that each group would not want to see the other one.

Brophy knew that the Russians were using the Blue Flame network to launder their money. The sources of their funds were various types of organised crime and the money that needed re-processing was of a semi-industrial proportion.

In the case of the Saudis, the money was genuinely industrial, but the source was more straightforward. Oil. And the motive was pure greed rather than a broad study of vice in the way of the Russians.

Amelia had selected an upmarket location in Kensington for

the forthcoming event. She knew that she would need careful orchestration because the two groups would need to see one another, think one another had the information and then watch as sparks flew. Probably quite literally.

There would be a couple of days delay before the players were in place and Amelia would also need some helpful support of her own for the situation she was about to contrive.

Chuck Manners had decided to move back to the surveillance station near the American Embassy. His position in the overall situation was improving.

He had met two of Jake's associates, had tagged them both with tracker chips and had followed them to a London location. One of them had moved on to a second location and then returned, and then both of them had headed away the Eurostar to probably Paris.

The long pause at one of the locations had allowed Manners to track down the disk drive from Jake's MacBook and he now had the code. He also had the addresses of both of the individuals based upon their movements around London. Next, he would identify their cell phones, and these would give him a better beacon on where they had gone to next.

Chuck Manners started with Bigsy and quickly found the cell phone information. It would take a while to trace it via telephone billing records to see where the most recent calls originated.

For the second cell phone, he had to trace firstly the address where the tracker had visited, then the electoral role, which gave three different names, and then the cross-check of the cell phones. Three different names, one female and two males. He now had a name - Clare Crafts. He would check this as well as David Jenkins, which he assumed was the real name of Clare's accomplice at the sushi bar.

The next stage took two hours to track down the recent

telephone records. He had access to the telephone billing systems, but as he suspected the calls were now emanating from abroad, at least for one of the phones. Strangely, though, the second phone was generating calls from the London area, most recently on the M4 motorway and then back in central London.

By returning to Bigsy's flat, Manners was now able to try phoning the convergent numbers in Clare's recent cell phone call list.

Manners called the cell phone number he had tracked, and was answered by Rick. Salesman Rick wasn't interested at all in Manner's attempt at accident re-insurance and soon hung up.

Now Manners just had to watch for Rick's departure from the flat. He now had someone who was communicating with Clare Craft's phone. Sure enough, Rick was heading out for the evening.

Manners followed, principally to get a sense of the individual's area of operation. Following him led to a club in Farringdon. The club was lively and loud, with two friendly-looking security standing outside. The person he was following was waved straight inside but as Manners approached, he was stopped. "This is a private party," said one of the overcoated men. "Do you have an invitation?"

Manners didn't and realised his chance to get inside was limited. "I'm here to see Jake Lambers," he hazarded.

"Well, please wait here," said the first man in an overcoat, "while we check this out."

Manners knew he could barge past these individuals but judged it unwise to create attention at this point. This line of enquiry was secondary to his main plan, which would be to follow the trail overseas and to locate whatever Collins was hiding.

Rick had turned around when he heard Jake's name but decided that it was better to keep going. Jake had been concerned about something. The last thing needed now was to find someone tailing him to the club.

Inside Fabric, there was a loud club track playing; Rick smiled when he recognised it as Clare's good friend Christina Nott with her distinctive vocals, but a mix of the song he had never heard before. Rick looked out for Jake and found that he was already seated at a small table in a rather comfortable part of the club. Fabric played loud music in the main bar area, but had a separate chill zone close to a restaurant, where Jake was seated.

Rick moved to Jake in the quieter area and immediately explained about the person who had been following him to the club.

"Hey Jake, I do get it about the car, the smashed up flat, and the danger and all. You'll have to explain it all to me some other time.   Right now, I think you'd better go," said Rick.

"I don't think you'll be safe here and the longer you stay, the greater the chance that the person following me will get inside here."

Rick's choice of an exclusive club night had introduced a delay to Manners. Jake examined escape routes and worked out that the kitchens offered the best route.

"Hey, I owe you, big time," Jake quietly slipped away, leaving Rick in the club.

Manners had worked out that the club was exclusive, but the restaurant was less so. By agreeing to book an immediate meal, he was able to get inside without further scuffle. Within five minutes, he was inside and looking for the person he had been following. He spotted him sitting alone, apparently reading a drinks menu. At that exact moment, Rick looked up and stared directly at Manners, then gestured to him to come over.

Manners was slightly taken aback by this but walked across.

"Hi," said Rick, "I think I saw you outside a few minutes ago? You were asking about Jake Lambers? He is a friend of mine, or was."

"That's right," said Manners, "I was hoping to say hello to him."

Rick smiled, "I don't know how well you know Jake, but he has left the country now. He moved to Canada. I think he has a job over there - Toronto, I think."

Rick made as if to get up. If he had managed to sound convincing, he knew he would not be able to stand up to any form of cross-examination.

"Thanks," replied Manners. He didn't believe what he was being told but decided he would be better to simply disengage from this line of enquiry and instead to start the tracing of Darren Collin's secret.

Manners decided to leave the club. As he walked away, Rick let out a sigh of relief. He would stay for at least another half hour and then tomorrow phone in sick to his office, thereby giving Jake a longer period with his car.

Manners had decided to follow the trail now – Jake Lambers was no longer relevant to him, but the address in Zurich was now critical. He would be moving his centre of operations to the location identified by the information on the hard drive. It was Zurich. The main thing he would need to do would be to ensure that whatever was stored in Zurich would get destroyed. The trail to the old empire required to go cold. Anything to do with Jake and his accomplices could be handled as an afterthought.

Manners still had the backpack containing the new laptop on which he had copied the data from the hard drive. He had already copied the content of the hard drive to a backup and then stored it in a locker for safekeeping. The laptop was a useful asset for the next stage of his job, which he would take as carry-on luggage for his flight to Zurich. He headed for Heathrow airport and stopped overnight in a nearby hotel, prepared for the first Zurich flight early in the morning.

Secure grip

As Clare and Bigsy left Darren Collin's Zurich apartment, they said to him that they thought he might not be safe staying there. If they could find the location, then so could others.

Collins said that he had been very meticulous with his camouflage plans and that he had spent a great deal of money setting up his identity in Switzerland. No-one could find him, and it was because he had given the information to Jake that had made his location traceable.

Clare and Bigsy didn't look all that convinced about Darren's cover story, as they left the apartment. They had enough information now to go to the UK Police and to start getting some protection set up for Jake as well as the pair of them.

They also had information about a serious money laundering ring, which they were confident would create interest from the UK police. They decided it was time to make their way back to the United Kingdom, but now they were reasonably sure they had not been followed, they would speed their return by catching a flight from Zurich's airport.

They left the apartment, hailed a taxi and climbed in. Another taxi one pulled up outside the apartment. Bigsy and Clare did not notice Manners getting out, and Manners did not see either of them. Their own taxi moved away as Manners walked towards the apartment block.

Manners quickly located the apartment from the website address and first pressed the buzzer for Suite 9.

"Is that you again?" Came a voice and the buzzer clicked as the door opened.

It was too easy.

Manners was now on his way to the apartment, which he would see if he could enter undetected.

As Manners approached the landing, he saw someone looking out of the door of a room, which he realized was the apartment he was tracing.

"Hello," he said, "I'm looking…," then he realized the person he was talking to was Darren Collins.

At the same moment, Darren recognized Manners. It was too late. Manners had Darren in a secure grip. He pushed him into the apartment and, holding his head down to the floor with one hand; Manners glanced around the apartment.

"Right," he said sharply," Do as I say, or I will start by breaking both your arms."

Darren agreed to comply, not sure at this point whether he had any options. "I am going to ask you a few questions," continued Manners, "I need the truth."

Manners released his grip on Darren, but stayed alert. Darren saw his angle.

"Okay," agreed Darren, "But consider this, I have a substantial amount of money hidden away in computerized systems. I don't know who you work for or how much they pay you, but

I promise you, I can beat just about any offer.

"In return, I need to know that you will work exclusively for me and act as my protector. I don't need you to be around full-time; I need to know that I am safe."

Manners was astonished by this situation. Here he was, grappling with someone he thought was already dead. He was there to find out whatever secrets had been hidden and to take the information to his masters, who were themselves part of the underworld.

The person he was threatening was trying to bargain with him. Bizarre, but on the other hand, the emotional response of the person he threatened seemed real.

Manners was going to take some minutes to decide the course of action.

In the taxi, Clare and Bigsy were commenting to each other at how good they were getting at problem-solving. Darren Collins had told them overtly about how the money laundering worked but also how the cells were linked together only as needed. This gave a remarkable resilience to surveillance, hacking and other criminal pursuits.

Because Darren had identified two of the business cells operating adjacent to his own cells, he could perform cross-checks of who owned what.

At Zurich airport, Bigsy and Clare waited for the plane and talked about the whole situation.

They needed leverage to try to build a position protected from threats to themselves or Jake. The information about other Blue Flame nodes could be the basis of their protection. They needed to get a situation where they could declare their hand and not be derailed by other possible assailants.

Inspiration

There's more to life than being a passenger
– Amelia Earhart

Brophy considers a new name

Amelia Brophy had chosen a small and rather exclusive hotel, for the roundup of the Russians and Saudi Arabians. She wanted the event to create damage and some casualties and she was going to arrange that she was apparently included in the ensuing carnage.

The Russians already thought she was dead, and the Saudis would soon do so soon as well. But her actions would also eliminate some of the people who had been aiming their bullets at her.

This situation had become personal.

She had checked the venue, which had several important features. There was only one primary forward way in. There was a short glass tunnel canopy leading to some manned double doors. Inside, there was a small and discreet lobby, and the other side of the lobby was first a bar and then a restaurant. The whole place was dimly lit and the focal area was a large cocktail bar area. At maximum, the bar would hold twelve tables worth of sofa sitting groups and the restaurant around fifty, with an area near to the back which could be screened off.

Her plan was simple. She would invite both groups to the restaurant on the same pretext that she had the data that they required. She would find a way to introduce them to one another, which would be like lighting the touch paper on a giant firework.

She could not predict whether there would be an immediate violent interchange between the two groups or whether they would discreetly leave and avoid confrontation.

She needed confrontation and was arranging her luggage to be in the lobby at the time of the meeting.

This luggage would be slightly heavier than usual, because it would contain 4 kilos of K-PEX high energy plastic explosive, which she could detonate with a mobile phone.

Her plan involved leaving the place around the time that the two groups discovered one another. If they fought directly in the hotel, it was a result, if they tried to leave, it was also a result, because she would, in both cases, be detonating the K-PEX and creating a crater the size of the restaurant cocktail bar.

The ensuing devastation would have taken out most of the Arabs and Russians, along with a number of innocent bystanders.

Included in this group would be a Ms Amelia Brophy, complete with passport and other identification. She would then be able to resume one of her other guises away from the mess of this situation. She decided that she quite fancied a poetic sounding name.

The plan was pretty simple, something she preferred. The Russians and the Saudis were already on the move, from Riyadh and from Cannes.

High above this scene twinkled a low earth orbit satellite. It had been monotonously tracking five Saudi Arabian mobile phones for several weeks.

A trigger alarm now created an email in Langley, Virginia. Four of the Saudis were on the move, together, to Riyadh's airport and then after going off the air for six hours, the signals had re-appeared in London.

Another email flicked across to GCHQ, Cheltenham, UK.

The monitoring post for UK counterespionage and terrorism was about to activate some special forces.

Manners makes a new friend

Manners had wondered for several years about what would happen if ever anyone made him the offer he could not refuse.

An offer to insulate him from the complicated life he had led since he left the army as a hero. He had not intended to get involved in semi-military protection of high-end criminals. But there was a buzz related to the activities unlike anything he could get in civvy street.

He had been through typical jobs after his honourable discharge from active service. He had asked directly about working through further special services, but there had been budget cutbacks that meant the best he was able to do was get outplacement which led to a mid-ranking job in a bank. This role had been madly inappropriate, and through an ex-contact he had ultimately fallen into his current line of work.

It had a lot going for it; travel, excitement, use of his skills, reasonably good money.

But Manners knew that he was reaching the end. He had plenty of experience, but there were other Armani suited professionals now on the market. There were slim-waisted girls with high calibre protection skills and large calibre guns.

He needed to move to a new plan and Darren Collins could be it.

"Let's talk," he said, putting Collins into a chair, showing him a large knife which he slid from behind his jacket and then saying, "do you have some coffee?"

For an hour, over two cups of coffee, Manners and Collins discussed a new business arrangement.

Collins had money stashed away from the business he had been running. It was mainly the money that had caused the Arabs to challenge him when they had visited his office. Collins had not been losing money; he had been swindling extra funds, which now formed the basis of his escape parachute.

"There is so much money, I have a problem hiding it," said Collins, "Yet it is only a small proportion of the money which the operation has been trafficking.

You can almost name your price," said Collins, " I need to be invisible, I need someone who keeps an eye on whether anyone is showing interest in what I do, and maybe some invisible protection."

Manners understood. It was the type of silent protection offered to ex-Presidents and senior politicians.

Not flashy like pop stars or menacing like gangsters, but just quietly efficient. He could do this and do it well. He would enjoy doing it, and because Collins wanted to keep an international lifestyle, it would still give travel.

Besides, Manners knew enough of the 'community' to be able to re-construct a past for Collins and himself and make them blend unobtrusively into whatever background he chose.

"Five million dollars and a regular monthly paycheque," said Manners. Collins laughed, "I think we have a deal."

They shook hands and Manners relaxed slightly, but still kept a grip on the handle of the hunting knife.

Hammered out

In London, Fredriksson had been patient with Dillon. There had been legal matters to resolve, and Dillon's lawyers were good. He had expected fly-by-night legal support, but Dillon had chosen wisely.

The main terms of the deal were hammered out, without significant changes and they were at the point of signing, along with an individual schedule to handle the first few days of the process during which the new systems and legal entities would ramp into production, along with initial transactions flowing through the system.

They had arranged to meet again, this time in a secluded office in the city of London, close behind the Law Courts.

Fredriksson was amused to consummate their deal so close to the traditional legal powers of the United Kingdom.

The deal was far from conventional. Fredriksson was ostensibly alone for this meeting also, but had nearby backup, in case anything untoward was suggested.

Dillon had arrived with legal brief in tow and probably also had further people out of sight. For the central part of the meeting, it was Dillon and Fredriksson. For the signatures, additional legal support attended for both parties.

The papers were signed, and a new node, covering around half of the old Collin's empire, was created. It would take another three days for the system to reach capacity.

Dillon left, instantly a multi-millionaire and with a rate of personal growth of wealth outstripping most people on the planet. Fredriksson smiled; another cog replaced in the broken machine.

ZRH -> LHR (J Class)

Trying to get from Zurich to Heathrow on the first available flight in the morning meant that Bigsy and Clare had to travel Business Class. It was nearly ten times the amount they would normally pay for the same journey with their own money. Nonetheless, they were pleased to get the seats and pleased to be able to spend a few minutes in the British Airways lounge at the airport.

In hardly any time, they were back over London, a bright early morning giving a view of the one-time London Millennium Dome, now sponsored by a mobile phone company and a clear landmark of London from the air.

As the wheels finally touched down with a skid and a screech, Bigsy and Clare looked at one another. They had another busy day ahead of them vastly away from anything they knew from a week ago.

As a priority, they were going to link back up with Jake. They needed to communicate and to find out what had been happening. After the seatbelt lights binged out on the ground, Bigsy flipped his phone on and called Jake. A few rings and Jake answered.

"Where are you?" enquired Bigsy.

"At Clare's," came the reply. Jake had used his own instincts to stay hidden. As his own place had been turned over, in a way he didn't fully understand, and then Bigsy's had been broken into, Jake was running out of places to hide. Clare was away, and as Jake had helped her move in, he remembered a key on his key ring; something he'd always meant to return but never got around to doing. Strangely, he'd got an almost sentimental attachment to it, something he'd never mentioned to Clare.

"I hope you don't mind," he continued.

"It's fine," came Clare's response.

Bigsy and Clare headed for Clare's place. They used the underground and mused that the journey from Zurich was only about twice as long as the journey from Heathrow to Central London.

As Clare opened the front door of the flat, Jake came towards them, and they all found themselves hugging one another, which was not their normal behaviour at all.

"OK, so what next?" questioned Bigsy.

They needed to find a way to bring this runaway situation to a sensible and safe conclusion.

"...but, can we make any money from it?" questioned Bigsy, "We have spent rather a lot". They all looked at one another.

Faux synchronisation

The security services message passed to GCHQ triggered some other events. As well as the four Arabs travelling to London, it also logged Fredriksson's move to London. This created some serious speculation that something would be happening.

The Serious Crime Unit had been notified, because of the suspected links of the four Arabs with oil shipment related crime and the separate investigations about Fredriksson related to his relationships with suspicious business practices.

Fredriksson was, himself, open in his movements, and the SCU had never been able to directly link him with any of the situations that had occurred in the past.

It now looked, however, as if there was a synchronized approach of both groups to London.

Of course, the real reasons for the link was not related to Fredriksson and had been the effect of Amelia Brophy's phone calls, but this had heightened the sense that there was something about to happen.

In a separate investigation, UK Customs had picked up a key Russian entering the UK and seen that two others accompanied him. The whole entourage from the Cannes meeting with Amelia Brophy were in London because two of them had flown from Cannes earlier in the week to attempt to eliminate Jake Lambers.

Converging on London were now both the Saudi Arabians and the Russians. They were known by the UK authorities and both planning to meet Brophy separately in the same restaurant in Kensington.

The authorities considered that there might be a meeting between the Arabs and Fredriksson and were going to take no chances in case of foul play during the session.

A separate trace was in progress towards the two Russian assassins who had killed the police officers Trueman and Green. Death of a cop was particularly bad in the eyes of the London Police, and so the heat had been turned up.

The Vauxhall car damaged at the crime scene by the Russians had been discovered and because the Russians were expecting a more straightforward get-away they had been much less careful than they should have been about breaking into the car. They had made the most basic of mistakes by leaving clumsy fingerprints on the vehicle.

These had meant the Russians could be identified. Both already had diplomatic status in the UK. Their biometric scanning was on file, and so the police had been able to identify them both.

Because of the level of suspicion and linkage to the murder of two police officers, special powers were granted to set up a five-person tracking operation on the two Russians. The botched-job Russians had not suspected the hunt which was in progress.

Run with it

Bigsy and Clare were starting to explain to Jake some of the information they had obtained from Darren Collins.

Jake told them that once he had realised how deeply he had become involved with the money laundering process; he had also identified that UK authorities would be severely challenged. Challenged to either round-up the ring or to offer him protection in the aftermath of any investigations and trials.

Therefore, Darren had decided to break away from HMRC for his own safety and to use the money he was processing to set up some separate funds so that he would have enough money to be able to disappear at some point. He needed to withdraw from his employers in Her Majesty's Government and the various shades of criminal that he was investigating.

That was when he started to devise his three-stage plan. He wanted a) a lot of funds b) someone entirely anonymous for be able to report the situation independently and c) identification of his successors in the laundering business in case of his replacement.

Bigsy and Clare understood this and that the meeting with Jake was a way to pass the information from Darren to someone else relatively random. By not having a pre-defined chain, it reduced the chance of being traced and would have broken the link to Darren.

Darren had been stealthy but methodical about discovering the way his businesses had linked with others. The official reason he was doing this was as part of his investigations, but he had rapidly seen the information as useful bargaining collateral if things got tough. He had discovered that the operation was truly global with a blend of illicit and legitimate businesses to cover tracks.

So Darren had started to look at the companies with whom he interacted. He looked for the ones that were legal and straightforward, but also looked at companies that were similarly complex in the way that his own company operated. These were the companies most likely to be further 'nodes' in the laundering operation.

On this basis, Darren had shortlisted the three companies most likely to be close copies of his environment and then had made contact with each of them. Darren had ruled out the applicability of one, and this had left two, where, in principle, there was a good fit.

Darren had investigated the possible organisations and already knew the person running one of them. Although the companies in this organisation were somewhat dubious, there was something about their construction that made Darren think the organisation was not a convincing fit as a substitute for his own.

Someone formerly unknown to Darren operated the other organisation. His name was James Dillon, and he moved in some of the same circles that Darren frequented. Darren's position had been propelled upward by the significant injection of cash from his business, but before that, Darren and James Dillon's paths were somewhat intertwined, even if they didn't know it.

Darren had worked out that Dillon was probably a target for a similar role to the one he played. He didn't know how it would work, whether Dillon was 'in waiting', perhaps already recruited and maybe even operating on a small scale. As someone on the inside, it had been made very clear to him that he should not ask questions or try to find out who else was involved or how processes outside of his own companies would operate.

That had made Darren Collins' job much tougher, because he had needed to find out about things he had been expressly asked to avoid. His information was somewhat inconclusive, but he had told Bigsy and Clare his suspicions and supplied them with a large amount of data about the companies operated by Dillon.

In the discussion in Zurich, a simple deal had been cut. Collins had handed over the information which he had, related to what he supposed was the creation of the new node. He'd suggested two ways that this could be used back in England.

The first way was to provide the whole set of evidence to the police and let them take over.

The other option, if Clare and Bigsy preferred it, was that they could do something directly themselves with the information. In the course of this, Collins had told them about the Arabs, Manners and Fredriksson as well as the lead to Dillon.

Darren said he didn't now have a preference. The only condition from him was that whatever happened should not provide any further references to him. The faking of his death earlier had been effective, and he did not want any resurrection of old facts.

So Bigsy, Jake and Clare were now working out an angle on the best way to use the information they had.

They knew about Darren, the triangle of trade, the probability of Dillon as the new recruit and the great level of danger if they made wrong moves.

So they started to describe some outcomes.

"Look," said Clare, "I'm not greedy in this, but if there is a way to recoup our cost, or maybe a little bit more, then we should do it.

"We also need to stop the hunt for us by the 'blue flame' or any of the other organisations."

"We also need to keep the police out of the way while we get the basics sorted out," said Bigsy;

"They are bound to doubt some of what we tell them, in any case, and we don't want to be held up in police processes when we need the ability to move fast".

All three nodded their agreement; they were going to run with this a little bit longer.

Clothes Match

They decided they would make contact with Dillon, but they needed to do this in a way that would ensure Dillon was reasonable.

They decided they would need to do this by intimidating him in some way and that the most natural way would be to imply that they were involved in the shadowy organizations themselves.

"We need to make ourselves look legitimate, in some way," said Jake, "otherwise we will be brushed off."

"So why don't we become part of a Serious Crime undercover unit?" suggested Clare, knowing this may be a crazy idea. "We could scare Dillon and get him to co-operate in some way."

"Duh.," answered Jake, "Now you are crazy".

"But wait a minute," said Bigsy, "Look at the three of us - a computer geek, a journalist and a graphic designer. If we can't come up with a convincing cover story, then nobody can..."

Clare agreed, and they started to create the background that they would need to persuade Dillon to co-operate. Jake was to write a couple of fake news stories, which he could then get worked into a copy of a magazine mock-up. Clare was to produce a relatively wide range of identity forgeries and a couple of unique photographic mock-ups. Bigsy was asked to participate in some electronic engineering.

The plan was evolving. They decided they would visit Dillon at his offices. One of them would pose as a member of the Serious Crime Unit. This would be Jake. He could look serious but was not threatening. If more heat was needed, then Bigsy was available as a background player.

They would need to persuade Dillon that they already knew his game and at the same time stop him from either telling the police or the underworld organization of their involvement. The plan was to keep Dillon as the intermediary in all of this process, and potentially to do so in a way that meant that Bigsy, Clare and Jake did not ever have direct contact with the 'blue flame' organization with whom Dillon and previously Collins had been in discussion.

Their plan was evolving:

Jake was to impersonate a representative of Her Majesty's Government (an illegal impersonation, of course).

Jake would call Dillon and tell him that there was the need for an urgent meeting and that it had to be off-site, away from Dillon's offices. He should say that this was a matter of grave importance and Dillon should follow instructions and to not discuss this with anyone else.

In case he was challenged, he would be able to quote Fredriksson's name and could use the sad situation of Lucien's death as a way to illustrate that the situation was very real.

Clare was creating suitable identity badges and paperwork for Jake and working out with Bigsy how to make it look slightly used and battered. Clare knew how to do this by computer using Photoshop, but this needed to be real. Bigsy's solution was simple. "Give them to me- I'll put them in the back pocket of my jeans for a few hours". Clare smiled; she knew this would probably work.

Jake was working out how to look the part for when he met Dillon. He decided that one of his more sober interview get-ups would probably be best. Jake knew, as a journalist, that 'playing the part' when he met people often gave the best results. If he wanted to befriend them, he would try to match their style.

If he wanted to be a formal journalist he had different clothing to match. The problem was his current lack of wardrobe following the encounters at his flat, which he had still not re-visited. He would need to go shopping and acquire some suitable items.

Bigsy was assembling a lapel camera, like the ones used in the best spy films. He carefully sewed a small module into the lapel of Jake's jacket. The thin wires would run through the lapel and into the pocket, where they would re-connect to a recorder.

It was almost undetectable and gave them a camera and recording capability for Jake's meeting. Jake would press a button at the start of the meeting, and the camera and microphone would spring into life.

Universal

"Every instant is a new universe."

— Joan Tollifson, Nothing to Grasp

Staged

Clare had called Dillon. It was like many busy people, where a personal assistant screened him. Clare was half expecting this and made several calls within two hours.

Finally, she added the magic name Fredriksson to the conversation. As if a curtain had lifted, she was suddenly through to Dillon. This had a dual benefit. They now also knew conclusively that Darren Collin's speculation had been correct. Dillon was involved; otherwise, the reference to Fredriksson would not have worked so well.

Clare now explained the need for a meeting with Dillon away from his office. She did not expect him to agree to this automatically, but when she laid on the pressure about the grave nature of the situation and the need for special care, Dillon eventually agreed.

Clare had selected a quiet location for the meeting. It was a restaurant in Millbank, close to the river Thames and part of a recently modernised hotel.

The critical criteria were that it needed to be at ground level, that it needed to be bright (so that the hastily constructed video camera would work) and that it needed to be quiet enough to be able to record the conversation.

The respectability of the venue would also reduce the likelihood of a 'no show' by Dillon. Its convenience as a short taxi ride from his office was also in their favour. As luck would have it, there was extra melodrama because it was just around the corner from a seriously menacing government building, which had cameras around their walls and police guards and being on Millbank, it was less than ten minutes' walk to the Houses of Parliament. If anywhere was to be convincing for their story, then this was it.

They had arranged to meet at one o'clock in the afternoon, and Clare had stressed that there would only be a five-minute period during which the meeting would be 'on'. If Dillon was late, then the meeting was cancelled. This added further intrigue and a spurious air of professionalism. Clare and Jake knew this was all a bluff.

Bigsy took a room at the hotel, which was also the venue of the restaurant. They could use this as a short-term base camp. For the meeting itself, the plan was to use Jake as the member of the Serious Crime Unit and to have Bigsy on a nearby table in case anything untoward was going to happen. The preference was to keep Clare out of view and for Bigsy to only break cover in an emergency.

Jake and Bigsy had taken their positions at the table. Clare had used the name "John Hastings" for Jake, and all of the identity papers and other documents he carried used this name. The table was booked in this name. They all waited with bated breath for the due time, and Clare had been sitting in the hotel lobby keeping an eye on incoming people. There was an advantage to the front of this hotel because the big plate glass windows there gave an unrestricted view of people coming and going, and sure enough at around fifteen minutes before one o'clock, Dillon arrived.

Clare was able to take several photographs of Dillon through the window of the hotel before he walked into the lobby. Clare pulled a large winter hooded coat over her head and made as if to walk out of the hotel. She noticed that Dillon had made his way to the men's room and once the coast was clear, she slipped to the elevators and off to the room booked by Bigsy.

At around two minutes to one o'clock, Dillon approached the restaurant, spoke to the maître'd and was escorted to the table where Jake was sitting. It was right in the window of the hotel and faced out onto a side walkway, with a brick wall opposite. An occasional person was walking along the thoroughfare, mainly hotel guests cutting from the hotel's exit to the other side where there was a good view of the River Thames and the Embankment.

Jake stood as Dillon approached. "Mr Dillon," he started, "So good you could come along." He felt subconsciously as if he was speaking like a character from a John le Carre novel and hoped it was not too stilted.

"Hello, Mr Hastings," said Dillon, "This had better be good."

"Good is a matter of opinion," continued Jake. "Let me tell you what you are involved with."

Jake then proceeded with the story they had defined. Dillon listened intently whilst Jake took him through the key points. Firstly, Dillon had been under surveillance for at least six months, they knew everything about him and his operation. Jake handed over a couple of sheets of printout which were from the data provided by Darren Collins. It showed a few of Dillon's companies and some turnover data. Then he offered another sheet which showed a detailed breakdown of expenses from a 'sales visit' which Dillon had made to Paris a month earlier. The data showed the individual sales receipt, in the form usually used by an accountant.

"Suffice it to say we have this information for everything you operate," continued Jake.

"Anyone with access to our accounts system could have stolen that," responded Dillon. "It proves nothing- you'd better show me some ID before we go any further, and if I suspect anything, then I will be calling the police in moments."

As if to prove the point, he pulled out his mobile phone and placed it on the table. Across the room, Bigsy's eyes nearly popped when he saw this - the phone was an unexpected bonus. He felt in the small key pocket in his jeans and retrieved the old SIM from Jake's old phone.

Jake showed Dillon the identity papers produced by Clare. They did look good, but also a little dog-eared, which added a good sense of reality. Of course, it relied upon Dillon not knowing what a real identity document would look like.

"Okay," said Dillon, "keep talking."

Clare had been working in the hotel room. They had installed one of Bigsy's printers and Clare's laptop computer. She was downloading the photographs of Dillon's arrival. She added a few words to the image and then, still wearing the hooded coat, stepped out of the room and made her way outside the hotel. She carried her laptop bag and camera and made her way to the riverside of the hotel, pausing as she passed the window where she could see that Jake and Dillon were engrossed in conversation. She was able to do two things here, including taking a photograph of the pair of them talking, all of which went undetected.

Jake explained that Dillon was under surveillance, suspected of being already involved with the money laundering and would be tracked down if he joined the process via Fredriksson. His only chance was to co-operate with the authorities, and in return, he would be left alone. With the money he already had, and the money he could make from the down payment from Fredriksson, he should be able to disappear and reinvent himself. In return, the UK authorities would start to dismantle the money laundering operation.

Dillon would be able to stay disconnected from what happened, and this would give him the highest chance of survival. Otherwise, he could continue with Fredriksson and know that he would be caught. He could tell Fredriksson what he knew, in which case Fredriksson would probably make him disappear, like Collins and Lucien. He could speak to the police directly, in which case Fredriksson would find out fast and then he would be in danger, and Fredriksson would disappear. Frankly, his best bet was to co-operate.

"You talk a convincing story," said Dillon, "but this could all be bluff. How do I know you really have information and access?"

"Let's think," said Jake, "Firstly, I know about your company, to maximum detail; secondly, I have shown you my identity information; thirdly, I have told you easily checkable facts about Darren Collins and Lucien Deschamps; fourth, this venue, around the corner from a few rather 'specialised' establishments is no coincidence and finally, take a look outside."

Jake gestured over his shoulder. There was no-one there, just the wall, with a few tatty posters on it for various clubs and gigs. Then Dillon noticed them.

Four yellow posters in a row. "Ministry of Death - Live on Thursday," it said, "featuring DJ Dillon". And the black graphic overlay on the yellow poster was a picture of his face, his face a few minutes ago getting out of the taxi to go to the meeting with Jake. Clare had done a good job of making the posters.

"Excuse the theatricality," said Jake, "but my point is that you are an easy target at present". We want to make the situation go away. Only with your help can we guarantee your safety.

"I need a minute to think," said Dillon, "give me a moment."

"Go ahead," bluffed Jake, "But don't try to go anywhere, rest assured we have you under surveillance. We need to finish this conversation". Jake was used to interviewees sometimes needing a minute to think about an important revelation. When he had got the exclusive on pop star girl Rachitta's coming out, he had been through a situation just like this.

"Leave the phone here," he added, "and don't go making any public calls either."

Dillon walked away. He just needed a few moments to consider his options. He could run, call the police or just go back to Jake. At the moment, that did seem like the best option. He walked outside the lobby of the hotel to the foyer, where he lit a cigarette. A Camel.

Bigsy was delighted. He'd cleaned out Jake's SIM after he had removed it from the phone and would now replace the one in Dillon's phone with Jake's. The main reason was to get Dillon's SIM, so that they could check through the numbers. As Dillon walked out of the restaurant, Bigsy swung past Jake's table, lifted the phone and sat again at his own. A minute later he repeated the manoeuvre and then walked towards the exit from the restaurant, where he could see Dillon smoking. He paused and noticed Dillon finishing the cigarette and turning to come back into the hotel.

"A good sign," thought Bigsy.

Moments later, they were both seated again.

"Okay," said Dillon, "I'll co-operate. What do you want me to do?"

"It's simple," replied Jake, "You just need to do what Fredriksson asks, but at some point, you will need to supply some information to us." Jake was assuming that Fredriksson's approach to Dillon would be very similar to the way he had recruited Darren Collins. There had been a sizable down payment to Collins when he had started the operation and Jake had assumed that it would be the same for Dillon.

"What information?," asked Dillon.

"Let me advise you. When you are asked to participate in this, you should ask for two things. One is a twenty four to forty eight hour review period for the paperwork, and the other is a down payment of thirty percent of the initial fee. Fredriksson will agree to the first and may negotiate on the second. Almost certainly he will have a number of treasury bills to pay you the down payment, and he would probably be surprised if you didn't ask for something like this."

Dillon almost smiled; he had already told Fredriksson he wanted fifty per cent of the initial fees' up front' and the two of them had haggled this to thirty per cent. That was one point three million Euros, or in dollars, it was close to one and a half million.

"That is fine," said Dillon, "What else?"

"You will give both documents to us," continued Jake, "We only need them for forty-eight hours, but will need to cross-check them for DNA as well as any other clues to origination. You will get them both back. If there are any legal elements requiring amendment, we will tell you. The money represented by the Treasury bill will also remain yours."

Dillon was unhappy about parting from the contract and even more so from the money.

"Look," said Jake, "If you co-operate now, you will get all of the money and be forever de-coupled from this whole situation. Any other course of action will leave you exposed and under risk. We don't want the money; it is better for us when you disappear, and the money disappears with you. Her Majesty's government cannot be caught up in money theft."

Dillon relaxed slightly at this final point. If Jake was who he said he was then this was probably his best and safest bet. He was already in this too deep, and the credential from Jake seemed genuine.

"All right," said Dillon, "I'll go along with this; but if I suspect anything wrong, I will track you down and take you down,," he continued.

"Everything will be all right if you follow these instructions," continued Jake. They had both ordered Caesar salads, and both had pushed them around the plate during the conversation. The meal was an accessory to the main point of the meeting, but it was now clearly time to move on.

"Do you agree to do this?" asked Jake, "Because, if so, then we can use the papers to trace the route to Fredriksson and even further back. You will still have been paid the two sums for starting up in Treasury Bills and can then lose yourself."

"Our Government will be creating so much heat for Fredriksson and his accomplices that you will not need to worry about them again. And you will have four million Euros for your trouble. I think this is considerably better than being killed or put into prison, don't you?"

Dillon stood to leave. "You give me little choice in this matter, he continued. "I do agree to follow these instructions, but please understand that I have a great sense of self-preservation. Frankly, even from the start, this proposition seemed too good to be true, and so I am not surprised when it comes like this."

They looked one another in the eye and shook hands. Jake decided that Dillon seemed surprisingly likeable, and he wondered how he had first got mixed up in this situation. As Dillon left, Jake signalled to their waitress and then started to pay the bill.

Dillon was good for his word to Jake, and when he had visited Fredriksson the first time, the whole reason for the legal delays and the requirement for the down payment had gone precisely in the way that Jake and Dillon had discussed.

Less than fifteen minutes after the first meeting with Fredriksson in the Foreign and Commonwealth Club, in a nearby 'Pret a Mange' sandwich bar in Trafalgar Square, the contract and the treasury bill had been handed over to Jake.

Jake had walked out of the sandwich bar and climbed straight into a taxi. "Take me to Cannon Street," he had asked. Cannon Street on the edge of the area of Central London known as Bank. The area where all of the world's main banks had offices; Jake was about to pay one of them a visit.

The right kind of bill

Bigsy and Clare had been waiting for Jake to arrive at their meeting place. They had taken up residence in a Starbucks next door to Cannon Street railway station. It gave a good vantage across the road to McDonalds on the other side. They had decided to meet in a different venue so that if they were being followed, it would be fairly obvious. Not many people would first visit Starbucks and then cross the road to another shop selling coffee and food.

Jake's taxi arrived, and he stepped out, paying the driver from the pavement, before walking to the McDonalds. Clare and Bigsy followed across the road and looked at Jake.

"We have it," he said, pointing to the envelope already on the table in front of him. It contained the contract and also a separate sheet of paper bearing the title "treasury bill".

Jake, Bigsy and Clare had expected the Treasury bill to look something more spectacular. It was merely a series of computerised reference codes. As well as the code it also said that the bills were not matured (although they would be in two days). There were some simple instructions to 'sell direct'. It just requested the seller to log in to the account and to select the appropriate function.

It said that by providing the information, a request would transmit to the Federal Reserve Bank of Chicago which, acting on the Treasury Department's behalf, would offer the bill to different brokers and sell it to the highest bidder. The proceeds of the sale minus a seller's fee would then be deposited into a designated account.

Clare looked relieved. "It will be a lot easier for me to create the new version of the T-Bill from this information," she commented. She was firing up her laptop on the table in the McDonalds.

"We must move quickly," said Jake, "Firstly we need to make a good copy of the contract and the Treasury bill information."

Across the road was a Kwik-Call printing shop. They requested that everything they had in the envelope was copied and that Clare's additional item was printed.

Then they set off for the nearby banking streets of London and found a suitable commercial bank with a dealer desk. It was unusual to deal in person, but the bank was not phased by the request or the amount. Doing this in central London was a lot easier than in the provinces, although Jake, whose account was to be used, was asked for passport and other details. The nature of Jake's job meant that he always carried this type of information around and he easily provided the details requested.

"This will take around thirty minutes," said the bank employee handling the request.

Jake had decided it was better to visit the bank alone. If anything were to go wrong, he was the only one known at this point. He knew the bank systems would include comprehensive video surveillance.

Within twenty minutes, the bank employee came back with a serious expression on his face. Jake expected the worst, but the employee said, "The transaction is complete; the money is now in your account. Please sign this acknowledgment, which also includes details of our fees."

Jake was slightly numb as he heard this. Their plan had worked surprisingly well. They were now sitting on the best part of one point five million dollars.

In the meantime, Dillon was now without access to either the contract or to the money and was feeling somewhat exposed.

He had returned to his own office in the City because, on the advice of Jake, he had been asked to make everything look as routine as possible. Two hours later, a courier arrived at his office and left an envelope.

Dillon opened the envelope. It contained the contract, the Treasury bill codes and a typed note from Jake, which read as follows:

"You followed our instructions accurately. We have copied the documents you provided so that they are returned to you quickly for your processing.

"The legal document looks fine according to our own people. The Treasury bill has a hidden catch at present. It is highly discounted for the next two days and will only yield you ten percent of its face value.

"When it matures, it will have its full value so we do not recommend it to be sold at present.

"The attached Treasury direct information gives you further details about the options, but in our opinion, Fredriksson has been clever in giving you a guaranteed payment that you should only exercise after you have returned the signed contract."

The information about the level of discounting of the treasury bills was false, but Jake, Bigsy and Clare hoped it was plausible enough to hold Dillon from trying to cash the order for the next two days.

The attached Treasury Direct information also looked plausible, but with the minor doctoring to it performed by Clare, the description in the letter seemed to tie up with the 'facts' in the leaflet.

Clare had also used her graphics skills to make a minimal change to the coding shown on the master treasury information. It meant that if Dillon did try to access the information for a sale, then it would actually give an access security error.

This would look like a password transcription error, but would add a few hours to the discovery process by Dillon.

It was also a small enough error to make Dillon and Fredriksson hopefully think it was a coding error rather than anything suspicious.

Clare had changed a couple of Zeroes in the document into Eights. The computer coded form of a zero and an eight did look similar and this could be put forward as a plausible cause of an error.

In the event, Dillon took the letter at face value. He was more relieved to get everything back and assumed that the people he was dealing with were being demanding about releasing payment before the rest of the contract was signed.

And in any case, tomorrow he would make his second visit and get the other two point seven million Euros from Fredriksson.

Right now, he thinking about ways to stage his disappearance in the aftermath of the processes started by the gentleman he had met a couple of days earlier in the restaurant close to the River Thames.

Serious Crimes Unit

The combination of the National Security Agency in Langley, Government Communications Headquarters in Cheltenham, the London Metropolitan Police, the Criminal Intelligence Agency and the UK Serious Crimes Unit had been in liaison for the last two days. A sequence of events triggered, now causing a lot of attention to focus on London.

Unknown to Amelia Brophy, who was on her vendetta, the combination of Fredriksson's movements, the two clumsy Russians at Jake's flat and Amelia Brophy's calling to the Arabs in Saudi Arabia now created a cauldron effect in Central London.

The NSA in Langley had been able to easily track the four Arabs. Their American destination cell phones were equipped with the now legally standard issue GPS chips used in America. Fredriksson was somewhat unlucky. As a Scandinavian, he just happened to be from a culture where cellular phones are highly popular and had a modern and elegant Scandinavian model. It was a very recent design and also happened to have the American style GPS built in, officially so that new capabilities could be offered to the technologically interested Swedes, Norwegians, Danes and Finns.

Langley had been watching this group of five for some time, and the GPS had made this easy. Now they were in UK jurisdiction. They tracking passed to local authorities, who were tracking by both GPS and the local cellular network.

The American system was still superior and more selective than anything done via the phone network, which was more reactive, tracing things after an event instead of before it.

An incident room had been established in a set of offices close to Chelsea Police Station. The offices were officially overspill police offices, but because of the nature of the Chelsea area with its royal connections, these building were secured to a much higher standard than typical police stations.

They also had considerably more technology, communications and even access to heavy equipment from guns through to helicopters and armoured artillery than any normal cop shop.

There were the nearby Kensington barracks, the home of soldiers who, whilst able to ride around prettily on horses in arcane armour, also had some of the most high specification equipment of any modern army. And it was right on hand in Central London.

The incident room was now being run by a Chief Constable Dennis Wilson. Dennis had known Detective Inspector Trueman well, and in his mind he felt that the current events were linked with the recent shocking situation where Trueman and Green had been murdered. So the combination of his rank and only slightly revealed interest in the case ensured a suitably senior stakeholding in what was becoming a potentially major incident.

The visit of the four Arabs to London had been relayed at a high level after they had landed and cleared customs. They had all moved into the Dorchester Hotel in Mayfair, which was a typical haunt for such luminaries.

Fredriksson was also in a hotel in a similar area although since they had left Riyadh there had been no further communication between them.

The London police had separately been investigating the murders of two of their officers in a nearby part of London, and there were clues that two Russian 'heavies' were involved, which had led to their being shadowed as they moved around London.

As a consequence of Langley and GCHQ involvement, the UK authorities had arranged phone taps for the Arab mobiles, as well as for Fredriksson and the two Russian gangsters.

Now they were piecing the events together. There was to be a meeting between the Russians and an intermediary in the hotel's restaurant called Baglioni's. At the same time, a meeting between the four tracked Arabs and an intermediary in the same restaurant.

A professional operator was running the phone being used to arrange all of this. It had been used to set up the calls and meeting and then been disconnected and dropped out of the grid. Whoever was acting as co-ordinator was based in London but operating at a very professional level.

The Chief Constable selected Chief Inspector Donovan to run the processes for this situation.

Donovan was under a lot of pressure from various directions. In the Operations Centre (or War Room, as everyone was calling it), there were representatives from NSA, GCHQ, Met Police, the Army, Royal Protection Unit, Household Cavalry, and the Serious Crimes Unit. The Royal Protection Unit had already intervened, and the significant Royals were all out of town or currently being ferried by helicopter to Balmoral in Scotland.

The basic plan was to treat the possibility of something serious happening at the restaurant, but more likely the restaurant venue was being used to plan something which would then take place on another occasion.

The main possibilities under consideration were terrorism related. Either planning an attack or settling the bankrolling for something?

The direct location was an unlikely target for anything, so it was much more likely that this was a preparatory meeting. As the meeting was in London, there was also speculation that whatever was planned was more likely to be affecting New York, Paris, Frankfurt or another capital city.

If it was not terrorism, the other great prospect was financial in some way. This was Donovan's own personal favourite, and he linked it to the matters affecting the murder in the nearby Sloane Square art gallery, the killings of Trueman and Green in Kensington and now this meeting.

Donovan, along with everyone else, assumed that Fredriksson was involved in the situation and had no knowledge of the involvement of Amelia Brophy.

There were only two days from first notification to the meeting, and by the time the team had been mobilised, it was the day before.

Civilian clothed, Donovan had visited the hotel and restaurant and quietly informed the management that there was a severe problem. He had asked to see the guest list and the list for the date in question. In late November, on a Thursday, the hotel was not fully occupied, although from Friday and in the time leading to Christmas it soon became busy again. The stylish clientele was international. The hotel's room prices, to Donovan, were high even by London standards, so there was a mix of pop stars, fashionistas and 'IT' people who stayed there along with well-heeled Americans, Japanese, Russians and Arabs. An exclusive nightclub ran most evenings, and there was a very discerning admissions policy unless staying at the hotel.

Donovan was commandeering the whole restaurant for the evening of the meeting. He explained to the hotel management that he needed to do this but in a discreet way. He said the most straightforward way would be to say that there were two visiting people in the next few weeks and to imply that they were senior Royals. The location of the restaurant and its profile made this entirely plausible. The evening in question had several tables booked but was quite light apart from hotel guests who may book on the night.

Donovan considered this carefully; a lightly booked restaurant and last-minute restrictions may blow the secrecy with which his own people were being deployed. He decided to adopt a variation of the plan. He would book the rest of the tables and fill them with his own people. This could be a combination of police officers and military, but needed to be done in a way that didn't make it look as if "Mr Plod" was in town.

He decided to take all tables, keep a couple empty to not arouse suspicions and to arrange suitable small groups and 'boy plus girl' assignations in addition to the usual guests who would be present.

The restaurant was quite small, and the capacity of the combined restaurant and bar area was less than one hundred people. To minimise confusion and capacity within the bar, Donovan decided he would have a large section reserved for a small private party. He was sure that the Household Cavalry would be pleased to oblige for this and could easily simulate a sporting victory or something similar which would allow them to play to type without needing to bring too many outsiders along.

Donovan realised that this was a potentially career-enhancing or career-limiting situation. The sheer profile was about as high as it could be; he had required paperwork signed by the Home Secretary and the amount of select units involved was about as serious as it gets. The Chief Constable had inserted him into the process as the operation leader. All goes well, and he could soon be a Superintendent. If it went wrong, he may be worrying about whether he would have a pension.

There was also a maximum level of security imposed over this process. Those involved for the next two days were being kept away from other officers and individually briefed about security. In addition to the British involvement, there was also a veritable array of special advisors from the United States.

Another stage was some special equipment installed into the hotel. This was less problematic than they had expected. The hotel was already wired for full camera observation and there were an above average number of door and general security attendants as part of the hotel's high-quality image. The Italianate staff were particularly attentive and stylish. Adding directly to their front of house number would be difficult.

Donovan decided that changing waiters or bar staff would be too difficult and quickly detected. Instead, he would arrange for high coverage from the available tables and that their placed people would carry any necessary surveillance gear. It was also essential to only enable any special technologies after the guests had arrived; otherwise, it was very likely that they would be detected by a sweep of the room by one of the security people accompanying their prime visitors.

The preparation was intense both inside and outside of the restaurant. Across the road was the edge of Kensington Park and a nearby gate to enter the park. Just the other side of it, on the edge of the broad footpath, two large Portacabins were being moved into position. This was where the reinforcement firepower would be housed. Three Chevrolet Trucks and a Mercedes van were parked behind the Portacabins and were unloading grey gunmetal and green and brown cases into the back of the Portakabin units.

Party Time

And the whole world has to
Answer right now
Just to tell you once again
Who's bad?

Bad – Michael Jackson

Quiet evening in Kensington

Amelia Brophy had checked into the hotel linked to the restaurant. She was also checked into the other cheap hotel about one and a half miles away. At the new venue, she was Ms Foster. She was still using Brophy at the other hotel.

His initial check-in was with just a small holdall. She would be bringing the rest of his baggage by taxi later. The rest of her baggage, in the other hotel, was already wired with the K-PEX plastic explosive and a phone detonator.

She could phone her case from across the road at the point she wanted to cause the devastation. She walked from the hotel to the street and looked around.

A park and some construction work opposite. A busy street was leading to the Kensington High Street. A tube station. A side street with a National Car Park. The car park was about 5 minutes on foot. The car park would be her means of escape. She would need a rental car, position it as close to the exit as possible, even if it meant re-parking.

She needed to know that both groups were in the restaurant and then to introduce them to one another. They would both suspect a trap, and this would be the point where they would start to make for the door. That would be when she would trigger the device. She would already be outside, across the road. She would then walk to the car park and make a casual escape while the confusion continued. Then head north by car and aim to finish at Manchester airport by midnight. Amelia then had most of the planet in reach for the following morning. She already had a reservation at the SAS Radisson, which was part of the airport complex.

Her hire car was delivered to her original hotel, and she drove it directly to the car park in Kensington and parked ready for the main evening events.

Everything was now prepared. Donovan had his men in place. Amelia Brophy was in the hotel. Her luggage was to be picked up by taxi and transferred to the new hotel. She would ask the concierge to leave it downstairs because she would be leaving the hotel shortly.

By seven p.m., the Russian group arrived at the hotel. They seemed in good spirits and regarding this session as a routine meeting. Although they were supposed to be collecting important data, none of them seemed particularly guarded or cautious. They took up their table and ordered some vodka immediately. It looked as if they had already been drinking earlier or at least that the security men supporting the group seemed particularly well oiled.

The Saudis arrived around forty-five minutes later. They also arrived in stages. Two suited men came first and walked around in the restaurant before the others arrived. They noticed the Russian group but did not take particular notice, other than they were particularly noisy.

Amelia Brophy had expected the Saudis to be late. Time

worked differently for people from the middle-east and delay was mainly to emphasize their importance. The security men called on their mobiles and then waited by the front doors of the hotel for the Saudis to arrive. A short time later two stretched S class Mercedes arrived. They both had darkened windows, and the four Arabs emerged. They all wore western suits and moved quickly to their table in the restaurant.

Amelia was outside of the dining area in the bar during this process and across from a noisy party of sportsmen, who seemed to be celebrating a recent rugby victory. She guessed they were military, based upon their height, haircuts and ways of addressing one another.

Donovan had watched all of this. He, too, was sitting in the bar in a good control position to see what was happening. He could see the Russians, he could also see the Saudis, but more importantly, he was looking for Fredriksson or anyone else carrying out observation. This was made simpler because around half the people in the bar and restaurant were supplied by him.

There was additionally a table of six banking types in mid celebration, presumably of a big city deal. They may have been acting, but their language and interaction seemed realistic enough for them to be genuine. There were a few couples, who looked as if they were genuine, but then again, so did a couple of his own units. A group of five Japanese in the bar waiting for a taxi seemed unlikely, and a large mixed family group who had come in from the street for a drink also did not seem very plausible. He was interested to see their reaction to the bar bill for their drinks in a few minutes. This left four individuals seated alone as his main marks.

One was clearly waiting for a girlfriend or partner, one was reading a book, and the other two were looking around. Donovan had spotted Amelia in particular because of her attractiveness and an attentiveness to the goings-on in the rooms. She had also taken what Donovan regarded as a 'control' position in the room. She could see everything yet could easily blend into the surroundings. To Donovan she was the prime. He noticed that the person was also making several phone calls.

Donovan was now hyper-alert. In addition to the calls, he could see Amelia approached by one of the hotel staff. Donovan could see that there was an arrival of luggage at the front door. The person he was watching was giving instructions to the doorman about the luggage. Donovan had stood and could make out that the instructions were to leave the luggage in the lobby entrance. The intimate size of the hotel meant that the lobby faced across towards the bar and to the restaurant areas.

Donovan saw the woman making another call. He noticed one of the Saudi phones ringing, and the Saudi take the call. Something was in play.

Then Donovan saw Amelia putting down money and starting to walk out of the restaurant. One of the Russians had looked over and appeared to recognize her.

There was a shout, Amelia continued to walk as the second Russian also stood and then pulled a pistol from a holster under his jacket.

Both he and the other Russian were taking aim on the person leaving the hotel. As she left, he looked long at the luggage.

Two shots rang out, and then almost instantly another four.

The Russians had missed Amelia and were now both on the ground courtesy of the Metropolitan Police. Several people in the restaurant screamed, and a couple ducked low to the floor.

Donovan looked to the luggage. He'd seen that look from the woman. He was convinced the luggage was involved in this.

A bomb.

He ran towards it as the general commotion broke out behind him. The Russians were reeling from firstly their own group firing on someone and then their security being breached.

The Saudis took a different view. They did not break cover. Their two security men pushed them into a corner of the room and then edged them along wall to a side door marked "Fire Exit".

Donovan was running towards the cases, hoping that no-one would fire upon him. The Russians seemed to have been neutralised, the Arabs in the room were trying to leave. Everyone else was part of the operation.

If the cases were a bomb, he had limited time to get them outside.

He had luck. They were stacked in true concierge fashion on a wheeled trolley.

He ran at the cart and pushed the whole thing along the floor towards the door of the hotel.

To his surprise, the footmen at the door opened it as he approached — years of training. The trolley continued on the walkway to the street, and then out of control across into the road, where it toppled to a crashing halt as two taxis braked heavily to avoid it. Donovan waved to everyone to clear the area. "Bomb," he shouted.

Inside the restaurant, there was still chaos. The remaining Russians were attempting to make their way forcefully but without firepower to the front door of the hotel, but they found themselves faced with significant declared firepower from other guests in the restaurant.

The Saudis had done better. Their exit through the fire door had been successful, and their cars were on hand to pick them up. Unfortunately, they had not expected a battery of armed police officers to be waiting at the top of the street they were trying to leave.

Amelia had done the best. Her departure was some twenty seconds ahead of the main alert. The initial gunshots and deployment of the armed forces inside had taken a few seconds to create the external reaction. As she left the hotel, two people had been stepping into a taxi. She had joined them, demonstrating the power of showing the tourists her rather expensive pistol.

The taxi had pulled away and she had then abandoned it about three hundred yards away, by the end of the road leading to the Car Park.

She was outside the cordon that was rapidly tightening around the hotel. Her priority was the car, then the explosion. It took her another minute to get the car to the exit from the car park, then she turned right and then left as she moved rapidly away from the area. She reached in her pocket, picked her phone, selected the speed-dial and pressed. Two seconds later she heard the explosion. She was already three-quarters of a mile away.

Back at the hotel, there was complete chaos. Donovan had used his radio to issue commands.

"Bomb Alert! Bomb Alert!

"If you are inside the hotel, stay there. If you are in the street, get away from the hotel entrance. Stop the traffic for one hundred meters on either side of the hotel right now. Do not approach the cases and trolley in the street, it's a bomb."

Another forty-five seconds. The inside of the hotel was controlled, The Russians had surrendered. The Saudis were outside protesting innocence. The police had stopped the traffic. The area was cleared.

There was a sudden noise of glass, then a loud bang, then a pressure wave and heat. The bomb had detonated.

Outside, it had done damage to the street and windows, inside it would have demolished the entire building and maybe the block. The street was fairly wide where the explosion had taken place. There was a small crater and blast damage, but altogether less damage and disruption than anyone might have expected. The blast could travel upwards without meeting resistance, and so a lot of its deadly force had been expended in creating a blast against nothing.

Everyone around the area looked at one another. They knew this had been a close shave. One of the Saudi security people immediately said, "We should leave the area. This could be one of several."

He had good terrorism training, but Donovan was sure that this was all there was. Whoever had just escaped had planted this as one chance. Two Russians had recognized him but were both dead now. It was not Fredriksson and looked like a professional freelancer - a woman. She would be hard to trace if she was outside of the hastily assembled cordon.

Indeed, Amelia Brophy, now Ms Jennings, was already approaching the coned road repairs leading to the M1 to head north to Manchester. Under the chair, nearest to where the bomb had initially been sited, was a passport and wallet with Brophy's documentation inside. If all had gone to plan, she would have been considered amongst the casualties. Now she was just disappeared, but as the two Russians who had previously tried to kill her were also dead, she had officially ceased to exist.

Donovan surveyed the scene. Two unoccupied burning cars. A crater the size of a small roadworks, but not very deep. A collection of dazed soldiers, security men and police. More mess than he had hoped but a lot less than there could have been. On balance, he would get promoted.

Endings or beginnings?

The events unfolding in Kensington were blissfully unknown to Fredriksson and Dillon, or to Jake and his companions.

In parallel, Fredriksson's second meeting with Dillon was taking place, again at the Commonwealth Club. Fredriksson knew that Dillon had cashed the first set of treasury-bills. The contract had been returned, the company processes were being established and Dillon was receiving the other three and a half million dollars starter fund.

Dillon was confused when Fredriksson mentioned that the treasury-bill had already been cashed. He knew he still had the notes and the codes ready once what he believed was a discounted time-period was finished.

Fredriksson moved the conversation along: "Here is the next three point five million dollars and these are already deposited in an account for you. We can resolve what has happened to the previous payment, but frankly, this will all seem insignificant in a few weeks when the main processes are up and running."

Dillon smiled wryly. He thought he might have been double-crossed on the recent transaction but either way, he was probably safely in pocket. If the unexpected Serious Crime Unit visitors had been genuine, then he would pocket the down payment, and maybe even the second part.

If his visitors from Serious Crime had been fraudulent, there was no way he would mention this to Fredriksson, because it would expose his complicity in the attempt to trap Fredriksson. Indeed, if they had been lying to him, then the original scheme with Fredriksson was still on, and he stood to make a lot of money from the new arrangement.

And, with the goods and services being virtual, the emphasis on proving the connection to anything illegal was still going to be a tough call.

Dillon considered the 'margin' on the transactions was as high as it ever could be - less Fredriksson's cut of course, which in any case was taken off the top of the deals as they flowed. Fredriksson also reminded Dillon this would be good business, as long as Dillon did not get careless in the way that Collins had. If he did, then retribution would be swift.

Dillon expected to be contacted again by Jake and at that time would be required to hand over the rest of the evidence so that Jake's organization could speedily take down Fredriksson's organization.

Back at the Travelodge near to Heathrow, Jake, Bigsy and Clare sat together sipping complimentary instant coffee from two cups and a tumbler. They all knew that the story to Dillon was made up, but that Dillon had almost wanted to accept it.

Jake, Bigsy and Clare had swiftly taken $1.5m dollars from Dillon and but at this point Dillon did not know this for sure. That was the attraction of bearer bonds and Treasury Bills. They were like high-value banknotes and untraceable after the transaction.

For Jake, Bigsy and Clare, they now had a rather large seed fund of money. If they never met Dillon again, there would be almost no way that Dillon could track them down. Dillon had no real background about Jake other than the fake story that Jake had given during the meeting.

The Travel-lodge was a suitably anonymous location and here they were summarizing what had transpired in the last few hours.

They had located Dillon, persuaded him to give them the deposit money from Fredriksson.

They had persuaded Dillon that Jake was from a special Government Department and that Dillon was already under surveillance. If they melted away from Dillon, they would not be traced. They didn't think Fredriksson had a lead to them either.

They knew that Manners was mainly interested in tracing Darren Collins's information and that this was part of another plan. They were still completely unaware of the existence of Amelia Brophy.

Their actions had, inadvertently, kept them away from the police. Their delays at the start of the week, when they had gone back to Bigsy's and the revelation from Jake that there were some extra aspects to all of this, had meant that they had never got as far as the police.

"What about the way that Lucien was killed, the robbery at Bigsy's and the big scene at Jake's?" started Clare; "We can't assume that the people chasing Jake have finished it," she continued.

"I will need to go to the police," said Jake, "They are bound to want to question me about Lucien. I'll need to play it very dumb. No one will believe how much has happened to us in the last couple of days, in any case, so I can just say I've been working on a story, from on the road. We also need to think about the other people that have links with us now. Some of them may be a little upset."

"Yeah, we're probably clear of Dillon and Fredriksson, but the original killer is still around, and we don't even know who he is working for.," added Bigsy, as he paced the small room in the Travel-lodge. He was looking anxious and started fiddling with the TV remote.

There was a loud bang. "Bigsy!" called Clare, "Turn it down!"

Bigsy had switched the TV on, and it was on a very loud volume setting. He fiddled the controls," Oops, sorry!"

He started noticing the programme. It was a news report, from Kensington. It was describing the events of the afternoon.

"This is Sebastian Walker, from outside of the Baglioni hotel in Kensington London."

"Today we have seen dramatic events unfold as police surrounded a suspected terrorist cell and then, in a lightning shoot-out, two of the suspects, both armed with rapid repeater pistols, shot on police and other innocent bystanders in the middle of the hotel lobby."

There was a cut to video footage of the hotel and some of the signs of devastation. There were the all-too-familiar signs of police blue and white tape in most of the camera shots.

The report continued, "In addition to shots fired inside the hotel lobby, there was an attempt to detonate a bomb.

"An unidentified onlooker pushed the bomb, contained in two suitcases, to the outside of the hotel. It blew up in the street, apparently detonated by remote control from a mobile phone. Fortunately, there was no injury but a huge crater and many broken windows."

There was a cut to a Chief Inspector," We had received information about a meeting of certain individuals connected with international crimes. The hotel had been chosen and we had already created a cordon around the location. We were not expecting anything as dramatic as the events which unfolded, but we did have a full terrorist and armed response unit on hand in case things escalated."

"Our expectation was of a simple meeting between interested parties. In the event, it seems that one group may have set a trap for another group, both of whom we have reason to believe may be involved in some form of gangland war".

"So were both groups apprehended?" asked the TV reporter.

"We were able to take a group of predominantly Russian speaking individuals for questioning following the incident," replied the Chief Inspector. He knew what was coming.

"So, the other suspected group?" asked the reporter.

"We don't think there was another group present," said the Chief Inspector, "It looks as if the sources were wrong, or that the other group were tipped off."

The Chief Inspector knew that the original reason his team were at the hotel was linked to the Arabs from Saudi Arabia. As they had left the hotel by a side entrance into a waiting car, they had presented diplomatic passports and documentation which allowed them to be whisked out of the area, even before the bomb had exploded.

Their car had been heading out of Kensington in the same direction as Amelia's even before she had managed to collect hers from the nearby car park. The Saudis had headed directly back to Heathrow. Their priority was to be out of the United Kingdom well before the main debate started in the UK media. And because they had not directly reacted to the situation, there was no proven linkage of them with anyone else in Baglioni's.

The reporter finished the interview and the TV cut back to the studio. Another TV presenter started a discussion about whether Kensington was becoming the "Wild West" of London. Then a cut to a panel debate about what needed to be done with police powers and security to prevent things of this type from occurring in the capital city.

"Wow," uttered Jake," This has got to be linked with what we have been involved with! It looks like a Russian group, presumably Russian mafia, were involved with a meeting, probably about the creation of the new routes? And then someone has tried to blow them up. This is all completely out of hand!"

They flicked around the limited channels on the Travelodge TV. There was a Sky news channel also describing the events. They had found a couple of eyewitnesses in the street. They gave a different account from the police. They described mostly the same information, but also that they had seen someone running from the hotel before a police officer ran outside with the bags on a trolley. They had also seen some Arabs leaving a side exit from the hotel and getting directly into a large black car and then heading away through a police road block.

"So, Russians, Arabs, a bomb and shooting," declared Jake. "This has to be linked to the Blue Flame and the triangle of money laundering. It looks as if someone was setting a trap."

"You know what this means," said Clare, "The stakes have moved past any of us. They wanted Jake when they thought he had information from the Darren Collins interview. The fact is, the game has moved past that now. Whoever is involved in these acts is beyond the likes of Jake and his sound recording. We know it's not Manners; he has had at least two opportunities to get Jake."

"There has to be someone else or another group. And they are moving up the food chain. As long as they are not tied to the money we have recently borrowed, then I think Jake will be all right now."

Jake didn't look so convinced, and neither did Bigsy. "Why would they stop chasing Jake?"

"My thoughts," said Clare, "Firstly, they'd try to kill Jake to get the recording information. They may have needed to kill Jake to get past him to the information, but in the end they could walk right into his house and simply steal everything. When they didn't get everything from Jake's, they located Bigsy's and stole the backup disk from there. So, they had the data they needed."

"Second reason," continued Clare, "As a warning. Jake could have been working for someone and that would be a reason to kill him. The Kensington incident we've just seen is a much stronger warning than trying to bump off dear Jake, here. If you think about it, Jake didn't know much either, other than the code numbers from Darren Collins, and they had a finite life-span with any value."

"Thirdly, I suppose Jake could have seen the Arabs, and he would recognize Manners. So, Manners could have killed him, but didn't. It was the data, not Jake, that Manners wanted."

Clare stopped. They all looked at one another.

"So, in risk to reward terms," said Jake, "At the moment we have one point five million pounds and the people who gave it to us don't know who we are". The others nodded.

"We think that someone has been after me, but that I'm no longer of interest because the events have moved on." They nodded again.

"And if we take this to the police, we will need to tell them everything, including about the money?"

They nodded again.

"You know," said Jake. "At the moment I honestly think we are ahead - we have some unique combined talents, have maybe worked our way through this with some luck, but could almost certainly learn a lot about running private investigations".

"We also have a good starter fund," nodded Bigsy, "If the money is right, I think we have some unique skills and experience to offer," continued Bigsy.

"One for all, all for one," added Clare.

The triangle was formed.

Chapter Forty-five: Post

He flipped the computer switch and typed:

"If you like reading endings first, then this section is for you.

"The triangle was initially written as part of a one-month project called NaNoWriMo, which takes place every November. London became the backdrop, and the characters became real. There's already a sequel, and a few clues about it dropped into the pages of this opening piece.

"The novel is thin, so that it can be read in a single European round trip flight, but it covers the distance of a blockbuster movie and, of course, 'The Triangle' has multiple meanings inside the storyline.

"There's more in store."

Enjoy.

x x x

CPSIA information can be obtained
at www.ICGtesting.com
Printed in the USA
BVHW040756260120
570519BV00016B/722